AN AVALON ROMANCE

A SUITE DEAL
Sue Gibson

Jilted by her fiancé, marine biologist Lily Greensly retreats to the tranquil shores of Loon Lake to research indigenous fishes and help out at her family's rustic fishing lodge. But when she finds an enormous new-age hotel spoiling the view from her cherished inheritance—the tiny and pristine Osprey Island—Lily decides the Nirvana Hotel's handsome owner warrants closer scrutiny.

Ambitious hotelier Ethan Weatherall cut his teeth in the hotel industry and is determined to buy Lily's treasured island and convert it to a concrete helipad. Career-climbing, cosmopolitan Ethan cannot risk falling for a woman who could never be happy away from the wilds of nature. But it seems that boat may have already sailed as he falls into the deep end for Lily's sweet soul and independent spirit.

Lily must figure out a way to stop Ethan from destroying the tranquility of Loon Lake while trying to resist his charming city-bred manners. If she can't, there's more than just Osprey Island at stake.

A SUITE DEAL

•

Sue Gibson

AVALON BOOKS
NEW YORK

Published by Thomas Bouregy & Co., Inc.
160 Madison Avenue, New York, NY 10016

Library of Congress Cataloging-in-Publication Data

Gibson, Sue, 1957–
    A suite deal / Sue Gibson.
        p. cm.
    ISBN 978-0-8034-9905-8 (hardcover : acid-free paper)
1. Women marine biologists—Fiction.   2. Islands—Fiction.
3. Hotels—Fiction.   I. Title.

    PS3607.I274S85   2008
    813'.6—dc22   2008005922

PRINTED IN THE UNITED STATES OF AMERICA
ON ACID-FREE PAPER
BY HADDON CRAFTSMEN, BLOOMSBURG, PENNSYLVANIA

For Mom:
Spending childhood Sunday afternoons listening to you
reading Laura Ingalls Wilder, Lucy Maud Montgomery,
and Louisa May Alcott sowed a seed that blossomed into
a lifelong love of words. Thank you.

Heartfelt thanks to my great friends and thoughtful critique partners, Kait Rainey-Strathy and Marie von Rosen, and also to my sister, Bev Gibson, an eagle-eyed proofreader who accepts chocolate for payment.

A big thank you goes out to the Ottawa Romance Writers Association, a diverse group of amazing writers who provide one-stop shopping for motivation, workshops, and camaraderie.

I'm grateful to my editor, Faith Black, for sharing her credible expertise and helpful advice.

Finally, I thank Tim, Maggie, and Luke for their unconditional and unfaltering support.

Chapter One

Lily Greensly's canoe sliced through the cattails, their slight stalks easily giving way to the cedar
strip's slim bow. Tilting her face up to the endless
blue, Lily drew her paddle from the water and rested
it, dripping, on her knees. Cotton-ball clouds scut-
tled across an azure sky, and a smile crinkled the
corners of her eyes.

"I'm back, and I'll never leave you again," she
declared to the open expanse, her arms stretching
wide to include the stands of Ontario's famous
spruce trees that lined the shoreline.

The spontaneous declaration wasn't entirely
doable, she knew. After all, an occasional trip to
Toronto was an inevitable, necessary nuisance, but

1

the sentiment, seeded deep in her heart, was genuine.

A shift in the breeze bowed the sea of heavy-headed stems and filled her nostrils with the lake's familiar marine tang. *I could stay here all day,* she mused, leaning back against a stack of life jackets to watch a pair of blackbirds flit and feed in the cattails. But she knew it would be months before the Hideaway closed its cabins for the winter, leaving her time to wile away an afternoon. She sighed and thrust her paddle to its hilt, shooting the canoe out of Cattail Bay and into the open water.

Time to earn my other paycheck now anyway, she told herself, a familiar uneasiness creeping into the pit of her stomach. She understood the danger of earning a salary tied to a dwindling research grant all too well.

She stretched forward to tap the depth-finder's toggle switch and let out a long breath as tiny black images began tracking across the screen. The finicky depth-finder did double duty—transferred daily from the canoe to her fishing boat—and was easily her most essential tool. One she couldn't afford to replace.

A high-pitched beeping began to pulsate across the water. "Oops." Her hand shot toward the black box and the volume button. Last evening Merv-from-Cabin-One cranked the unit's volume, claiming his hearing wasn't what it used to be.

Deep in the marsh, a blue heron flapped its wings and began an undignified ascent from the bay.

"Sorry, Sam," Lily whispered, her eyes following the bird's ungainly flight up and beyond a ridge of jack pine.

She bent to the monitor and eyed a school of perch circling at the three-foot mark. Tucking a strand of hair behind her ear, she slipped off the clipboard's protective cover and added the data to a sheet already crowded with figures.

Now, that ought to do it, she decided, running her thumb across the edge of a thick sheaf of papers, before squinting toward the dropping sun.

Tackle boxes in hand, Merv and Ed were probably already pacing the Hideaway's dock, scanning the lake for a sign of their fishing guide's return. She smiled at the comic image and stuffed the clipboard into her pack. Grabbing the paddle again, she headed for home. Time to switch hats.

Soon the stark profile of Osprey Island's lone spruce poked into the horizon, and she shifted forward on the hard seat. Not more than a rough slab of granite fringed with juniper, her inheritance from Grandpa Greensly wasn't even home to the osprey any longer.

She scanned the shoreline. No sign of yesterday's

bread crusts, she noted with satisfaction. Predictably, the scavenging crows had bussed her picnic spot clean again.

Lately, she'd come ashore often. She'd munch through her sandwiches in glorious silence, far from the Hideaway's good-intentioned folk. If one more person tut-tutted their sympathy, patted her shoulder or recited an uplifting platitude, she'd scream. The fact that they all thought her ex-fiancé, Doug, was a jerk—that she could tolerate.

A familiar melancholy seeped into her heart, stealing the good of the moment. *No. I refuse to let him ruin another perfectly good day.*

Doug had shown his true colors when he'd produced his humiliating prenuptial agreement and then bolted when she'd refused to sign it.

In hindsight, signs of their incompatibility had been there all along. Last summer, he'd balked at coming out from the city for their annual fish fry. As usual, he'd laughed off the Greensly traditions as old-fashioned and corny. But back then, she was still clinging to the notion of true love overcoming all. "Humph."

She dug the paddle deeply to the left and the canoe surged ahead. The lake's newest landmark, its absurd profile jutting from the rocky shoreline, caught her attention. The locals, inspired by the hotel's alabaster walls, had dubbed it "the Wedding Cake." A flapping banner proclaimed the Nirvana Hotel part of *the* Weatherall chain.

She frowned as visions of tourists, more-dollars-than-sense types, tossing pop cans from speeding boats flashed through her mind.

Her hands tightened on the oak paddle, and she could almost hear her grandpa's voice admonishing her anxious thoughts, "Worrying never got anything done, girl. If something is wrong—fix it."

And he was right, she mused, chewing on her bottom lip. But first she needed to determine if the fancy Nirvana was putting Loon Lake in jeopardy.

Tomorrow couldn't come soon enough as far as she was concerned. As soon as the sun yellowed the eastern sky, she'd be on the lake, guiding the CEO of the new hotel to a walleye hot spot and hopefully getting answers to her questions. Like why did he book a fishing appointment before dropping in at the Hideaway for a visit? And did this big-city hotshot have an agenda that could harm the lake? She straightened her shoulders.

Nobody messed with Loon Lake. At least not on her watch.

Ethan Weatherall struggled to raise his wrist closer to his eyes. His stiff canvas sleeve gave way, cracking conveniently at the elbow, and he peered at his Rolex.

7:05 A.M. Right on schedule, he observed, and went on to do the math of his day's schedule. Yes . . . Barring complications, he'd see Emma tonight.

He repeated his glance at his watch. His much-heralded guide was four minutes late. Pacing the length of the concrete dock, he looked down to the jingling zipper tabs and flashing fishing lures dangling from his pants.

Callie, his shopaholic assistant, had ordered his pants and fishing gear from the glossy pages of an Outback Outfitters catalogue with her usual enthusiasm. But to be fair, he'd never even opened the canvas camouflage-colored bag Callie had handed him as he was heading out of the office.

He eyed his gadget-laden khakis doubtfully and turned to eyeball the distance back to his temporary office and his regular pants.

No way. Not enough time, he decided, and instead turned to study the magnificent building he'd commissioned. A glance around the construction site confirmed he was alone, and his burgeoning smile widened. *There's not a hotel anywhere that compares with this baby.*

Just a month to the grand opening and only a single, albeit critical, detail remained: the purchase of the scraggly little island out front of his hotel-in-the-wilds project.

He sucked in a breath of bracing air. He'd developed the Nirvana project from beginning to end, except for his father's last-minute interference—the proposed helipad on Osprey Island. Predictably, the older members of the board, R.W.'s cronies, preferred to call his father's meddling an inspiration. They'd overrode Ethan's original idea of cutting a deal with the small local airport and alternatively using the funds to purchase the scrub land behind the hotel for development of a nine-hole golf course.

Roland Weatherall had insisted that a helipad built on Osprey Island was essential to the success of an outback hotel. *Outback?* He shoved his clenched fists into his pants pockets, remembering the dismissive tone of his father's voice.

By plane, the Nirvana was only an hour from downtown Toronto. But short by only one vote and needing the final release of funds, Ethan conceded. History had proved it futile to face off against his father.

Shortly after arrival, he'd learned from the locals that it would be impossible to convince the Hideaway's renowned fishing guide to sell her island. He shot another look at his watch. He didn't understand impossible. Even Ms. Greensly's treasured slab of granite had a price.

The buzz of an outboard drew his attention to a small boat beelining for his dock and he focused on the lone female occupant.

Is that . . . girl . . . with the blond hair whipping back from her face Lily Greensly? He'd assumed she'd be of the hearty, robust variety. Suddenly he wished he was up against a man, someone . . . bigger, a player.

She cut the sporty runabout's motor just inches from his feet, a flourish of spray peppering his new "Mach III" deck shoes, and tossed a tie-line across the short distance.

She stretched to clear the seat of life jackets, and he envied the casual comfort of her faded Levi's and beat-up sneakers. A waterproof jacket, lacking any recognizable logo, was tied around her waist.

"Do you mind?" she asked politely, nodding to the small steel hoop cemented to the dock and the tie-line she'd tossed across.

I knew choosing Junior Entrepreneurs over the Scouts would come back and haunt me someday, he thought, hating that he'd momentarily slipped from the power position.

"Sure," he feigned smoothly, "no problem." A couple of quick wraps and a tug on his loop should do it, he decided, kneeling to block her view as he attached the rope to the ring.

He rose to one knee and thrust out a hand. "Good morning, Ms. Greensly. Your reputation precedes you."

"You obviously booked this session through my father. He tends to exaggerate my abilities, Mr. Weatherall."

He warmed to her honest evaluation. "Call me Ethan."

"It's Lily, then."

She was pretty. Bits of fair hair blew around her heart-shaped face. Clear skin, surprisingly pale for the outdoorsy sort, presented an Ivory soap endorsement for clean living. There was a quiet assurance about her. Not a girl after all, but a no-nonsense woman, comfortable in her own skin.

Her chin tipped upward and he found himself looking into a pair of eyes as blue as the lake itself. Dark lashes, free of the kind of stuff most of his dates layered on, swooped up and down as she inventoried his outfit. A tiny smile pulled at the corners of her mouth.

I knew it. I look like a fool.

"Hop in," she said without a trace of ridicule, "the sun's rising fast. We'll head for a spot where the fish are deep and hopefully hungry."

He clamored aboard and folded his legs into the space between the seats and wondered, is this little boat designed for two passengers? A pair of life jackets stowed between them suggested it was, and he settled on the hard bench seat.

One quick tug and the boat drifted from the dock.

Thumping and cresting back through its own waves, they crossed Greensly Bay in a surprisingly short three minutes. And they were headed straight for the island—a bonus he hadn't expected. *Perfect.*

She cut the motor near the craggy shoreline. "It's called Osprey Island," she informed him like a tour guide at a theme park. "Pickerel generally hold near the shoal in front this time of day."

"Excellent," he said, avoiding her eyes and accepting her offer of a fishing rod she'd plucked from a narrow rack attached to the side of the boat. Nothing to feel guilty about, he reminded himself as he wiped his palms on his crisp khakis.

Now all he needed to do was watch and wait for an opportunity. He was good at pitching ideas and settled in to enjoy the buildup.

"Give me a sec," she said, and began pushing buttons on a small blinking box.

Long before high-tech gadgets were the norm, he and his dad had fished on this lake. *In a spot a lot like this,* he swiveled and searched for familiar landmarks, *Father showed me to how to thread worms on a hook.*

He could almost taste the grape soda on his tongue, as the blurred memory sharpened. His father had laughed—right out loud—when his six-year-old son had stuck out his purple-coated tongue at a circling bird. Their family holiday at a rented cottage was supposed to have lasted a week, but business had pulled Roland Weatherall away after two short days.

"Ethan?" Lily's voice was, soft, as if she understood she was bringing him back from somewhere distant. "Choose a lure please."

He shook his head, and like a drawing dissolving into an Etch A Sketch, the memory faded, and he returned his attention to the job at hand.

Her tackle box flashed its wares as the five-level case expanded the width of the boat. The woman owned more lures than Outdoor Outfitters. He observed her pick and plucked a lookalike from the selection.

"Good choice," she noted. "A Mister Twister."

Ridiculously, his confidence grew with her offhand remark.

Lily's lure hissed softly as it arced high above a patch of lily pads. "See. Now you try. Remember, flick, release, rewind." She spoke slowly, as if to a child.

His brow furrowed and he inched forward on his

seat. Flick, release, rewind. The shiny lure zinged toward its target in a smooth line and sunk precisely where he'd intended, and he wondered, had she'd been watching?

Suddenly, he was ten again, poised at home plate, his hands glued to the bat, hoping his father was in the stands. Too proud to check the crowd, he'd run the bases, only scanning the home team's crowd after he'd touched home plate.

"Good cast, Ethan," Lily commented, bringing his thoughts back to the job at hand. "You've been holding out on me."

Again, he warmed to her compliment, knowing full well she probably said that to all her clients.

He smiled and turned to scan the lake for signs of civilized life. A tin sign tacked to a boathouse advertised gas and BBQ chips. Farther down, the Hideaway's graying docks poked quietly into the bay.

He watched as Lily alternately flicked, and then tightened her line, wondering, *Is this really what she does? Every day?*

"So what do you do out here? Besides guiding."

She looked up quickly and he wondered at the defiant flash in her eyes before she returned her gaze to the water. She sighed, opened her mouth to speak, then closed it, as if unwilling to put out the effort. "Not much," she finally offered up.

"Oh, come on," he needled.

"I'm a marine biologist."

A what? He studied her face again, searching for something he'd missed. Apparently she was much more than a capable, blue-jeaned fishing guide. Generally, it took far more than a pretty face to throw him off track.

Although Reg, the well driller, had slipped under his radar too. Turns out Reg had a master's degree in engineering and was an ordained minister. There should be a manual, he decided, *The Dummies' Guide to Rural Folk.*

"Fascinating field of work—marine biology," he said.

"Right now I'm working for the University of Toronto," she continued. "Mostly I collect data from the active spawning sites of indigenous coldwater fishes"—she paused to check the depth finder—"for my research."

"I see. Sounds er . . . rewarding." He dragged his gaze from her face and struggled to digest the new information. His pitch for the island definitely required fine-tuning.

They sat knee to knee, casting to the shoal and slowly rewinding their lures. The depth-finder beeped, drawing Lily's attention, and he was reminded of the second reason he booked Lily Greensly's services. Fastening his gaze to the tip of his fishing rod, he concentrated on catching a fish.

This is the stuff, he observed: bracing breezes, clean air, nature's best at the doorstep, the smell of juniper filling the air. Great copy for the front cover of the brochure, he decided as an unwelcome sensation filled his lungs.

He coughed quietly, casting a quick glance to the back of the boat and Lily. *Not now.* He patted down his cargos in a hunt for his inhaler.

"Are you okay?" Lily looked up, concern flickering in her eyes.

"I'm . . . great." He tightened his grip on his fishing rod. He'd pass out before sucking on his inhaler in front of her. He flicked the end of his fishing rod again and smiled away her concerned expression.

Life on the lake had etched fine lines at the corners of her eyes and he wondered if she even bothered with lotions and creams. A scattering of freckles tracked haphazardly across her cheeks and nose. Wisps of her blond hair lifted in the breeze and danced around her face.

The outboard sputtered, punctuating the silence with a fuelly hiccup before returning to its smooth purr.

He tipped his rod toward the motor. "So is that a

two-stroke or four?" he questioned, and knew that all his nights spent reading the Ministry's environmental reports had just paid off.

"We switched to four-strokes three years ago," she answered quickly, her tone intense and interested. "You know, I participated in a study where it was proved, conclusively, the four-stroke outboard reduced emission by—"

Lily's rod tip suddenly dove. In a fluid movement she adjusted a dial and began rewinding her shrieking reel.

"Quick, grab the net." Her eyes directed him toward the back of the boat.

He grabbed for the Lunker Limo secured to the side of the boat and waved it like a flag. "Got it!"

Craning over the side, he spotted a brownish blur, at least a yard long, slicing through the weed bed. "There it is!"

Lily's sneakered foot pressed against his as she braced for a fight, and he quickly debated his options. *Should I help? Or is that against some unwritten fishing code?*

She clung to the bending rod, a smile lighting her face, and he settled back to watch. Suddenly the taut line was limp, coiling loosely in the water.

Ethan searched the blue-green expanse for the fish but only found his own disbelieving face mirrored back. He waited for his thudding chest to settle before straightening. Trading stocks on the floor of the TSX had nothing over this.

"I lost it. Didn't set the hook fast enough," Lily stated flatly.

No excuses. And somehow he doubted she'd accept them from anyone else either.

A tumble of blond hair fell across her cheek, shadowing her eyes, as she set the rod aside and began to ransack her tackle box.

He shifted on the hard seat and fought an urge to reach forward and pat her knee. After all, she is a professional guide, he reminded himself, not a regular woman.

He watched her absorbed search and decided her looks went beyond ordinary. Glamorous? No. Refreshing would be a better description. And nothing like the women he dated.

Not that he'd had a date lately. Ever since they'd struck a shovel in Loon Lake's shoreline he'd been too busy and had way too much riding on the project to worry about the state of his social life.

"What's going on?" Lily's hand was cupped over her eyes as she looked toward the rising sun.

Warmth rushed from his neck to his hairline, and he quickly swiveled to follow her gaze.

A flat-bottomed barge chugged steadily toward

their anchored boat. *Already?* He glanced to his watch, surprised at how fast the morning had passed.

"Ahoy, Mr. Weatherall," a slim young man with shoulder-length hair called out through a megaphone.

The loaded barge continued to advance, an enormous wake rolling from each side. Lily watched in amazement as Ethan's hand rose in response.

"You know these people?" she spluttered.

He flashed a look of irritation toward the barge. "They're with me," he admitted, a trace of defiance edging his tone.

She straightened in her seat. The itsy-bitsy spark of appeal she'd been trying to ignore since she'd collected the tall, dark, and surprisingly young CEO from the Nirvana's dock sputtered unceremoniously out.

When she'd neared the dock and spotted her client, she'd been taken aback. Most CEOs were older, grayer, and had spent decades slugging it out in the corporate trenches before earning their stripes. But this man had stood, feet spread on the concrete, confidently claiming his space. Any woman would sit up and take notice. Even a woman completely disillusioned with the moral fiber of today's male gender.

"They're from my marketing division," he continued, as if that excused the interlopers from accountability and sensible boating practices.

Marketing? Questions hammered in her head. What had that to do with their fishing trip? Obviously he'd instigated this floating three-ring circus, but for what reason?

She sunk her arm to the elbow in the frigid water and grabbed for the anchor line.

Her first tug produced nothing, and she realized the anchor was stuck on the lake's weedy floor. Banking down her panic—*I can do this*—she crouched in the space between the motor and the seat and yanked with all her strength.

Ethan's body blocked out the sun, as his arms circled her frame. His large hands covered hers on the thick line, and together they lifted the line in heavy, wet lengths.

His life jacket's zipper tab pressed into her back as he continued to apply his strength, and she wondered briefly if he worked out. He obviously was a power player in the boardroom and his considerable upper-arm strength suggested he held his own in the gym too.

As the coiling rope piled at their feet, she decided, if nothing else, that he was a chivalrous man. She drew her hands from the line and tucked them close to her sides.

In seconds, he plopped the dripping anchor next to her feet, like a cat presenting his master with a juicy mouse, and slid back to his seat.

A little voice in her head singsonged, "He's trying to impress me," and she repressed a smile. Men were really just oversized boys sometimes.

Her fingers tightened on the pull-cord's plastic handle. She yanked hard, the engine fired, and she brought the boat around.

"Lily," he said, a touch of remorse deepening his tone, "I apologize for my employees' carelessness." He nodded toward the now idling barge. "I should've told you that Link, my photographer, would be joining us this morning."

Yes, that would have been nice. "Photographer?" she almost yelled.

"A high-profile corporate face on promotional material sells. Basically we need a shot of me holding up a big fish."

At least he has the good sense to be embarrassed, Lily credited, noting his sudden inability to look directly at her face.

Still, questions pressed for consideration. Why not just tell her father about the photo shoot when he booked the appointment? Why did he not mention it while they were fishing?

"Want the simple truth, Lily?"

"That would be . . . refreshing."

He tracked her hooded gaze until he caught it, full-on. His eyes locked with hers, probing past polite, challenging her to trust his words.

She held her ground, refusing to look away, before finally bobbing her head for him to continue.

"I hadn't considered how our market-driven decision would impact on your space. I won't make that mistake again."

His lingo-laden confessional confirmed her suspicions: He was a self-centered autocrat. One she'd like to dump, clanking pants and all, to the bottom of the lake.

"Mr. Weatherall," Link's voice implored through the megaphone, "we're losing ambience as the sun rises. Chop, chop."

Ethan held his questioning look, his eyebrows slightly lifted, waiting for her response. His mother must have been wrapped around his little finger, Lily thought, his boyish charm bleeding the strength from her anger.

He wasn't asking for the world, after all. Just a few pictures. Her fingers went to her windblown hair and she glanced at her stained shirt and frayed jeans. "But we don't *have* a fish," she squeaked out, seizing the inconsequential in hopes of dashing the whole ridiculous setup.

"Link can airbrush in a fish back at the shop," Ethan countered quickly.

Lily looked to the photographer. Link was leaping over reels of electrical line and slapping ineffectually at the swarming black flies.

This guy was in charge of choosing a fish for the brochure? Ethan's corporate face might very well end up next to a saltwater halibut the size of a dolphin.

"Don't you even think about printing any brochures without my permission."

"I appreciate that the integrity of the lake is a priority with you," Ethan said, sounding relieved. He extracted a legal form from his breast pocket and stabbed a finger at the final paragraph. "Prior to publication you'll have veto rights on the photograph," he reiterated, raising his flattened palm to halt the advancing crew. "You have my word."

Lily hesitated, afraid to trust his words. Her focus slid from the paper to his coffee-colored eyes. She met quiet integrity there, urging her to accept.

Lily lifted her face to the sun. Perched atop the spruce, she spied Sam, the lake's sentinel blue heron. He chomped contentedly on a yellow perch, seemingly amused by the chaotic scene below.

A giggle rose in her throat. It was all quite ridiculous, really. "I'll hold you to your word, Mr. Weatherall," she said, and reached for his pen.

"Okay! Let's do it," Link shrieked.

A generator growled to life. Tiny chickadees

fluttered from the arms of the spruce. Floodlights bathed the morning mist a pale blue.

"He's setting a mood," Ethan shouted over the rumbling generator. "We're targeting the 'upscale, hip consumer.'"

There was no way the great marketing wizard was getting off easy. She raised her hands in a gesture of helplessness and held an expression of confusion as he attempted to explain his tactics.

"Yuppies," he bellowed through cupped hands. "We want the yuppies to come. Escape the rat race, connect with nature"—the generator belched a cloud of toxic smoke—"in this unspoiled paradise."

Chapter Two

With Ethan safely returned to his dock, Lily set her sights on the end of Greensly Bay. The short ride gave her just enough time to compose herself before facing certain inquisition. She cut the runabout's motor and let the waves carry her boat in to the Hideaway's dock.

Just beyond the shore, the Greenslys' log home nestled into a spruce stand. A row of smaller log cabins lined a worn path that went on to disappear into the bush.

Jared Greensly rose eagerly from an Adirondack chair, one of six circling a stone fire pit, and hurried to meet his daughter. A red plaid shirt tucked into a pair of pressed green work pants signaled

52797

today was special; his favorite shirt was generally reserved for the opening day of pickerel season or the fall fair.

Catching her father's eye, Lily puffed a strand of hair from her face and rolled her eyes.

His eyes lit up, obviously anticipating a story.

"So? What happened?"

"You were right, Dad. They're big, they're bad, and they're ugly," she called out, wetting an oar to propel the boat across the final few feet of water.

"Well, that's not exactly what I said, Lily." Jared shook his head in mock exasperation.

Lily hopped from the boat to the dock. "The big and ugly part you've seen, but we'd underestimated the bad part a tad. Ethan Weatherall tricked me. It wasn't so much that he wanted to catch fish as he wanted to *look* like he was catching fish."

Jared raised his eyebrows and waited.

"He used my services to market his hotel. They're printing up brochures, promoting the Nirvana as some kind of yuppie retreat."

She waited for his reaction.

"Will your face and the Hideaway's boat be on this brochure?"

"I guess. But he's right there beside me, holding up a yet-to-be-determined fish."

Jared knotted the boat's line with practiced ease before straightening and turning to his daughter.

"Isn't any publicity supposed to be good publicity?

"Well, I suppose . . ." *Why does he always turn things around until he finds the good in a bad situation?*

"And isn't the best darned guide in the country front and center on a fancy brochure?" he continued.

"Daaad. Please stop saying things like that. It's embarrassing."

"Okay, okay."

Jared grew serious, "Any news about the 'wedding cake'? Get a peek into the hotel? Bet it's a doozy."

Lily paused briefly, acknowledging his sly change of subject. "No, but he invited me to stop by later today. Said he needs advice on a few things."

"Well, there you go. He's not too stuck on himself to ask for an expert opinion."

She shot a warning glance toward the smiling man.

Jared tipped the rim of his Tilley hat, "You'll have to fill me in tonight. I'm off to Buttermilk Falls. Got a meeting with Henry Faulkner," he said, tugging his cuffs into place.

Henry had been keeping the books straight for the lodge for thirty-five years.

It wasn't year-end yet. She'd wondered about

the old fishing boat that needed replacing and his decision to raise the weekly rate on the rental cottages.

A long sigh escaped from her lips. There was no point in even asking. Jared was the epitome of the strong and silent type, convinced it was his duty to protect his family from ugly realities.

Lily fell into step with her father's slower gait as they headed toward the guest cabins. "I'm taking Merv and Ed out again. Those two have fished hard all week. They're determined to make a good showing at tomorrow's fish fry."

Jared nodded in agreement.

She checked her watch. "I hope they're ready. I'm meeting Ethan at the Nirvana after lunch."

Jared grinned. "It's 'Ethan' already?"

Lily ignored his jab and hoped the heat suffusing her face would pass without comment. Her father had the annoying habit of assuming every age-appropriate bachelor became smitten with her on sight.

Jared's footsteps slowed to a full stop. "I've got an idea. Why not invite our new neighbor to the fish fry? What better way to get to know the man and his motives."

"Dad, really, he'd hate our party." The image of Mr. Brooks Brothers mingling with the Hideaway bunch was hard to imagine.

Jared's gaze fastened on his daughter's face, urging her to reconsider.

"All right. I'll ask," she said, "but I'm betting our little fish fry won't interest him in the least."

"So what do you think?" Ethan asked, one hand resting on a black marble pedestal, the other pointing toward the etched glass panels fronting the Nirvana.

The pride in his voice evident, Lily pivoted to absorb the room's ambience before replying. Some forty feet above, heavy oak beams not only held the structure together but anchored chandeliers of crystal medallions. Prisms of colored light sparkled throughout the space, as if a fairy had waved her wand and spread stardust everywhere. Aware of his gaze on her face, she took care with her reply. "It's amazing."

He nodded, obviously pleased with her answer. "Wait until you see the dining room. We worked with a Scandinavian designer to develop the opulent yet casual look the demographic is buying into now."

Lily recalled his earlier shouted reference to the "yuppies" he was so desperately trying to attract. Now apparently, in the Nirvana's exquisite lobby, they'd become "the demographic."

"But first, I'll show you my favorite suite." He

placed a hand on the small of her back and directed her to a bank of elevators. The warmth of his hand melted through her thin T-shirt and she slowed her steps to enjoy the courtesy. Her ex-fiancé, Doug, generally strode ahead of her, even on their way to pick out her engagement ring, she recalled. His habit of walking ahead of her was irritating, but she'd found it easier back then, in the throes of first infatuation, to blame it on her shorter legs than his bad manners.

They stepped in, and the elevator purred them to the top floor with the doors opening directly into the penthouse.

Lily's feet mired in the sumptuous carpet as her eyes absorbed the vista. The expanse of glass was repeated here, and Loon Lake glittered below like diamonds on blue velvet.

This must be how it looks to the birds, she mused.

Picking her way through the artfully placed décor pieces, she pressed her fingertips to the glass.

She swung to face him. "How much would it cost to stay in this room?" she blurted out. She slapped a hand over her mouth, embarrassed by her boldness.

"Not at all, Lily." Ethan waved away her embarrassment. "We're both in business. Upward of a thousand a night. Pretty standard for a penthouse suite in a hotel of this caliber."

Lily's eyes followed the shoreline, reveling in the familiar, until her gaze was jarred by the skeleton of an enormous steel boathouse just to the left of the docks. Uncompleted, the first few feet of the imposing building were sided with gleaming white steel. Granite cliffs, the muddy hue of November storm clouds, towered in a protective stance just behind, the resulting clash of color and form an assault on the discerning eye.

Ethan hovered nearby, rocking on his heels, obviously anxious to continue the tour.

"I knew you would appreciate this view. That's why I brought you up here."

"Thank you. It's magnificent and worth every penny," she added with a smile. "But the color of the boathouse . . . Is there some reason it's being built so high and er . . . so white?"

Ethan followed her pointing finger to the construction site below.

"I realize the hotel is white, and you're going for a match, but the hotel's glass alleviates the impact of the white walls. The boathouse, on the other hand, looks almost industrial. And unless you're expecting to house the tall ships in there, the height is excessive."

Ethan crossed the room and began riffling through a stack of rolled architectural drawings. He hurried back and spread a sheet open against the glass. "Here it is." He tapped the spot. "We plan to build office space up there for the marine staff and . . ." He focused on the fine print. "You're right. The white steel has been color coded to coordinate with the hotel's paint."

"All I'm saying is that I would have gone an-other way. Lower profile. Made it blend in with the rock." Lily's voice faded. "Too late now."

"This is the only suite where a guest can see the boathouse," he continued, a defensive edge to his tone. "And who would even notice a building way off to the left when the whole lake is out front?"

Catching her reflection in the glass before turn-ing to comment, Lily lowered a raised eyebrow. "What about when your guests are out on the lake fishing? Your stunning frontal view marred by that . . . thing." She poked the glass with her index finger.

"Okay, okay. Point taken." He grabbed for her hand. "Come on. There's a lot more to see." He scanned the room for a clock. "I'm taking a confer-ence call in thirty minutes, and I want to show you the brick fish-smoker we brought in from Norway."

She hurried to match his steps, embarrassed at how intrigued she was with the lifestyle of the rich and famous. He showed no sign of dropping her hand as he led her toward a Picasso reproduction hanging adjacent to the elevator doors.

He let go of her hand and began to explain the history of the painting, gesticulating for effect. She stuffed her freed hand into her jeans. Leaning in to hear the story of the colorful painting, she knew she was seeing the real Ethan Weatherall—a man born to the world of sophisticated art and fine living. His animated voice brought the artist's work to life and suddenly she realized—*I'm actually having fun.*

It had been so long since she laughed spontaneously, or for that matter even smiled without forcing her lips.

She watched his face light up as he talked about the guest list for the grand opening, and listened to his deep voice as he told how couples from China and Paris and the Prairies would soon fill the suites.

She smiled at his enthusiasm, happy today it was only the two of them—she wasn't comfortable in crowds.

Their tour ended on the docks. "So that's it," Ethan stated. "Of course, it still needs the finishing touches. The detailers come in and do their thing and then the Nirvana is open for business."

"Best of luck, Ethan," she said as she fumbled with the tie-line's knot and climbed into her boat. Amazingly, she actually meant it.

Do I ask him? He was leaving for the city now

and wouldn't be able to come anyway, she remembered.

"By the way, we're hosting our annual fish fry tomorrow. Starts at one. You're welcome to come," she rattled off. *There. I can truthfully tell Dad that I invited him.*

She turned to check the gas gauge, allowing him privacy to formulate his refusal.

"I hope I don't have to bring my own fish."

"I understand completely—" Lily looked up from the engine. *He was coming?* Her stomach flip-flopped. "Um, of course not," she mumbled. "You're coming?"

He smiled, and her resolve to keep her distance crumbled slightly. "Wouldn't miss it, Lily."

She liked the way he said her name, his voice soft and deep.

With trembling hands, she reversed out of the docking area, clunking heavily against the dock's bumpers. She shoved her tackle box ahead with her foot and rolled the throttle forward with her thumb.

Was it Loon Lake that was in jeopardy or her self-imposed ban on men, she considered as the boat took her into the mouth of the bay. Just because Doug turned tail when her genetic profile revealed she had a slight chance of becoming blind in her later years, it didn't necessarily mean all men were incapable of a real commitment.

The boat bounced across the choppy water and she fought the desire to look back to the Nirvana. The Friends of Loon Lake Committee did a fine job watchdogging the shoreline and the fish, but when it came to protecting her heart, she was on her own.

Chapter Three

Lily mingled with the Hideaway's guests, topping up glasses of iced tea and plucking empty glasses from tabletops. She'd traded yesterday's look, T-shirt and jeans, for a backless cotton sundress, and had gathered her hair up into a loose knot. Escaping tendrils already clung to the back of her neck.

Without a breeze to clean the air, wood smoke floated just above the rooftops. Twice she'd observed Ethan turn his back to his attentive audience and draw on an inhaler.

Her hands smoothed the light cotton of her dress. It was a different look for her and she hoped no one would comment. At least not in front of Ethan Weatherall.

A collective laugh drew her attention. Ethan stood a head taller than the milling guests who circled him like kids around an ice cream vendor. His white polo shirt and crisp gray pants fit his tall frame perfectly, better suited to an afternoon on a golf course, but spoke of success and confidence. His forearms already sported the beginnings of a tan and each time he consulted his watch, its golden band flashed a subtle message: I'm wealthy and tightly scheduled.

Ethan nodded his head in apparent appreciation as Merv-from-Cabin-One regaled the crowd with details of his morning's outing. Encouraged by Ethan's smile, Merv extracted his wallet from his back pocket. Creased photos of walleye and bass flitted to the ground. Ethan knelt to gather the pictures as the older man beamed his appreciation.

Earlier he'd sequestered her father by the barbecue for a good twenty minutes. He's working the crowd, Lily decided. *My crowd.* Her hands tightened their grip on the frosty glass pitcher.

"Lily, how are the salads holding out?" Marion Greensly touched her daughter's elbow and waved a hand toward the picnic tables, each one covered with a brightly colored vinyl cloth.

Lily scanned the Pyrex bowls. "Potato, half-empty, macaroni, hardly touched. Oops, Mr. Jenkins is scraping out the last of the caesar salad."

Last year her mother's fading eyesight regressed to the point of legal blindness. Lily and her father had happily taken on the job of describing her surroundings.

"Well, thank heavens I've got another batch made up," Marion said, her white-tipped cane clicking rapidly as she made her way up the path of interlocking brick.

"I'm right behind you, Mom."

Cooler air bathed their faces as they walked the oak-planked center hall and entered the kitchen.

Marion Greensly moved easily from the refrigerator to the counter. With one hand she withdrew an enormous bowl of romaine lettuce, counted over to the third bottle from the left and extracted a jar of homemade dressing from the door.

"It's going great, isn't it, Lily," her mother said, the heat and excitement of the day coloring her cheeks. "And your new friend, Ethan, is a big hit, isn't he?"

"You got that right," Lily muttered to her mother's already departing figure.

Lily watched as her father met his wife at the front door. With his arm resting companionably on her shoulders, he escorted her across the porch. When they reached the bottom step, the couple paused. Jared drew his wife closer and planted a kiss on her cheek. A pink blush suffused his wife's face and she laughed softly before slipping her free arm around his waist.

They made it look so easy.

"Real love smoothes out the rough patches," her father had explained to her after Doug had called off the engagement. Lily swallowed heavily and yanked open the refrigerator's tiny freezer door.

The cold blast cooled her frustration as she recalled how Doug had circled her shoulder with one arm and waved a thirteen page prenuptial contract with the other.

"Take the blood test, Lily," Doug had insisted, *"and we'll go on with our plans."*

Hoping it was his lawyer's idea, she'd laughed it off at first. "Come on, Doug. What are you saying? If the blood tests say I might someday lose my sight, like Mom, you'll take your ring back?"

"Wouldn't you want to know, if it was reversed?"

Her world had tilted. "I suppose it's something . . . but when I said yes to your proposal, I meant, you know, in sickness and health . . ." Her voice had faded.

"Lily." A long pause foreshadowed his reply. "It changes everything."

"It's a nice little spot you have here," a deep voice boomed.

Lily smacked her head on the freezer door,

knocking a tray of ice cubes to the floor. Slamming the door shut, she scrambled after the slippery cubes. Ethan bent to the task, rising with a handful. She nodded toward the sink.

"Are you all right? Let me have a look."

"I'm fine. Thank you," she said, retreating from his approaching hand.

She waved away his concerned glance and continued, "We're not stylish but our clientele is loyal. Keep coming back year after year."

The Nirvana's clean lines and spacious rooms were in sharp contrast with the Hideaway cabins' gingham and pine.

"Apples and oranges, Lily."

Her gaze slid to the tiny emblem discreetly displayed on the pocket of his country-club shirt. "Absolutely. Day and night."

Silence hung between them, demanding attention. Lily's gaze sought the western view. A ball of orange blistered the lake. Burnt-meringue tips of foam, too many and too fluid for the eye to understand, stretched across the bay. Crimson streaks backlit the sky, forecasting a clear day tomorrow.

Ethan's gaze followed hers. "Magnificent, isn't it?"

"Mmmm." Lily sighed. "Money can't buy anything that beautiful."

Ethan's brows furrowed. "Too bad the Nirvana

is on the opposite shore. I hadn't realized how spectacular the sunsets would be."

Lily recalled how he'd explained that every detail of a new hotel was researched thoroughly before breaking ground. Was someone's head about to roll?

"Most of your clientele will be up early to fish, right?"

"Yes. I believe so." He eyed her with interest.

"Don't you remember the sunrise over Osprey Island when you and I were fishing?" Lily waited for his response.

A smile stretched across his perfectly straight teeth. "I certainly do. Priceless."

"I'd call it a gift, actually. But you get my point."

"Touché. And by the way, I faxed your comments about the boathouse to my architect."

"You did?" *The comments where I totally trashed his design?*

"He's agreed to do a mock-up in earth tones and with a lower profile. I had my construction foreman take me out on the barge. You're right. Lake approach is an entirely different consideration."

Lily's neck and cheeks warmed under the compliment.

"Thank you." She raised her grandmother's crystal pitcher and gestured toward his glass.

"Sure. Homemade I presume?" He slid his glass forward.

"It's just regular tea and ice cubes. Oh, and I popped a couple of mint leaves in too. It grows wild on the north shore."

He leaned in slightly before speaking. "Another one of your secrets revealed."

Her heart skipped a beat. *Dad, you're so in trouble.*

His face only inches from hers, his mint-flavored breath warmed her cheek.

"Go on." She knew her father's stories were rooted in love but they tended to be of a personal nature. Like the fact that she was single, and would make a fine catch for some lucky fellow.

"It's been a day of revelations," he continued, the beginnings of a grin twitching the corners of his lips.

"Oh really?" Lily pressed into the edge of the Formica counter and steeled herself for the worst.

"A fellow . . . Chuck, I think, told me that every Wednesday at dawn, you pick dew worms from your lawn into a bucket . . ."

He paused for a breath and grinned.

There's more?

"And his wife Hazel recalled the night you spent in your boat monitoring spawning trout. She said it rained, but said you were a real trooper and stuck it out."

"Is that all?"

"That's all I got for now."

She exhaled. It could have been much worse.

"You're a fascinating personality, Lily Greensly," he said. "My sister would love you. She has high regard for the unusual."

The unusual? What did that mean? Her insecurities kicking in, she wondered, did he think she was some kind of curiosity, a quirky personality whom his sister, no doubt a bored socialite, collected to show off at parties?

She straightened her shoulders. "Guiding is a service we Greenslys have proudly offered for over sixty years, and the environment, especially this environment," she said with an expansive sweep of her free arm, "is something we *all* should worry about."

A melting chunk of ice shot from the counter as her hand slammed down.

He pulled back. A glimmer of confusion flickered in his eyes before they shut her out, like a curtain dropping at the end of a play.

He reached for her hand, but she hastily tucked it into her pocket. "I'm sorry. I was joking. I completely respect your loyalty to the family business."

She nodded her head, indicating a grudging acceptance of his statement. He couldn't have known he'd inadvertently hit on a hot-button topic. While studying in Toronto she'd grown tired of explaining and defending the rural lifestyle to her urban classmates who'd bought into the country bumpkin stereotype.

"Sorry too. I'm a little sensitive when it comes to my work." She knew she'd been a rough on him, with the whole schoolteacher admonishment thing. Delaney was always telling her to tone it down a notch whenever she got up on her soap box.

Ethan stepped back and retreated to the far end of the counter. "Well, I'm sure our paths will cross again. I'll just go and say my good-byes to your parents now," he said.

She swallowed a lump the size of a peach as his empty glass clinked into the sink and he turned to leave.

Her sandals plopped a dismal rhythm as she headed up the back stairs to change. She paused on the landing and listened to his footsteps fade and wondered why she even cared that he was leaving.

Ethan retreated down the dim hall. *Well, I sure blew that.*

Oddly enough, Lily's disappointment in him

stung more than the fact that he wasn't any closer to owning Osprey Island. Canceling yesterday's meetings and his flight back to the city hadn't netted him the island, so why didn't he regret the wasted time?

He continued to stride toward the door. A row of paintings, obviously commissioned in a time when no one smiled for a portrait, depicted what he assumed were stiff-lipped Greensly ancestors. He squinted to read the spidery script in the corner of the largest painting—THOMAS GREENSLY, 1927.

The man stood on a rocky outcropping with a string of fish dangling from his raised hand. A lone tree stood in the background, its peak topped with a cumbersome pile of sticks and long grass. Ethan rubbed the cloudy glass carefully with his finger. There was no doubt. It was Osprey Island. And judging by the date, the man would be Lily's grandfather, who, according to the locals, gifted his only grandchild with the island.

His gaze dropped to the threadbare welcome mat by the door and traveled through the screen door out to the dented aluminum boats rocking against the docks. Was Lily even safe in those old things?

The Hideaway obviously needed an infusion of cash as much as he needed the deed to Osprey Island, and he made a mental note to increase the offer.

Taking the porch steps two at a time he headed toward Jared Greensly. Now there was a man of reason, the polar opposite of his volatile daughter. Maybe Lily could be persuaded to part with the island if Jared sanctioned the sale? Lily's respect and affection for her father was obvious.

Ethan had little experience with affection but he understood parental authority perfectly.

"Leaving so soon, Ethan?" Jared said.

Ethan glanced around. The crowd had thinned, most heading to their cabins. Merv's earlier declaration, that the biggest fish were landed at dusk, had been followed by a collective nodding of heads. And judging by the age of this crowd, a snooze was in order before heading back out on the lake again.

"Afraid so, Mr. Greensly. My pilot is waiting at the Buttermilk Falls landing strip. Not all of us are lucky enough to live out here." He glanced about the grounds and pictured himself sinking into one of Jared's big Adirondack chairs, drink in hand, waiting for the sun to drop off the horizon. And Lily would be there too.

Could he stay? No way, he reminded himself, Emma was counting the days.

"We're so glad you dropped by, Ethan," Marion chimed in, linking arms with her husband. "You said your good-byes to Lily while you two were in the kitchen?"

"Ahh . . . yes. Lily mentioned the Friends of Loon Lake Association earlier. When," he asked, pulling out his day timer, "does the group meet again?"

Jared tipped back his Tilley and rubbed his brow for a second. "Normally tomorrow night, but it's canceled until Lily gets back from Toronto. She's got a meeting at the university. Handing in her research papers and trying to drum up support for her next project."

Lily in his town, his territory? His pulse quickened. Another chance to talk to Lily? Instantly, he decided against speaking to Jared about Osprey Island. Lily wouldn't appreciate being treated like a child or anything that smacked of manipulation.

He clicked the black case closed and pulled a small card from his breast pocket and directed Jared toward the toll-free number. "When you know the date of the next meeting, could you leave a message with my secretary, please?"

As he turned to leave he caught sight of Lily picking her way through a scattering of pinecones, a life jacket dangling from each hand. A breeze fanned strands of blond hair from her face and he thought she might be the prettiest woman he had ever seen.

Okay, here goes nothing. Encouraged by her faint smile he edged closer and cleared his throat.

"Lily," he blurted out, "fly away with me to-night." *That didn't come out right.* He was definitely losing his touch. Too much fresh air or something.

Jared and Marion's heads swiveled toward his voice. Apparently as comforted by Lily's look of horror as he was embarrassed, they crossed the porch and disappeared into the house.

Chapter Four

"Ethan! You're back," Emma called out, the excitement of her twin brother's return spotting her cheeks with pink. She hurried across the condo's slate-tiled floor on her tiptoes and snuggled into his outstretched arms.

That's my Emma, Ethan thought with affection, *always complaining about the cold floors but never remembering to wear her slippers.* Her tousled hair brushed his chin and the familiar smell of his sister's apple blossom shampoo meant that he was home.

Man, it felt good to be back. "You were asleep when I got in last night, Em," Ethan said. "Told you I would be home today."

She drew him over to the dry-erase board that

hung in the kitchen. "You were gone too long. Look at all the *x*'s we put on the calendar."

Thirty white squares, filled with tiny black lettering detailing his itinerary, allowed Miss Scott to locate him at a moment's notice. Heavy black lines obliterated the information. But he knew what he'd so confidently jotted in yesterday's spot: *Purchase Osprey Island.*

His grip tightened on his leather attaché case where the offer lay undisturbed among his papers. Lily's polite refusal to fly to Toronto with him last night had left him with no opportunity to present it. And it was an excellent offer, he reminded himself, but timing was everything.

"I know I was gone too long, Emma. But soon we'll go there together. You'll love my new hotel. When you look out the windows you can see the lake and acres of trees, and when the sun rises it comes up all at once. A huge ball of sunlight that makes the lake sparkle. Like diamonds."

He suppressed the urge to tell her about Lily. And what was there to say, really? *I met a fascinating woman who thinks I'm the bad guy, bent on destroying the environment—and her life.*

Emma clapped her hands. "When can we go, Ethan?" She searched his face for an answer with chocolate-brown eyes that matched his own. "Please, can we go today?"

I shouldn't have said anything, he realized as guilt rolled through him. "Not today, Emma. I've got to go to the office right now. But we'll have our Friday night dinner out. I promise. Anywhere you want to go," Ethan said, edging toward the door.

"Mamma Mia's?" she responded immediately, predictably choosing their favorite Italian restaurant.

"It's a deal. See you later," he called out, knowing full well the odds of him returning before midnight were next to none. The reinforced steel door clicked shut, and he stood for a moment listening for the automatic locks.

Over the low hum of the rising elevator he heard Miss Scott's voice encouraging Emma to get ready for a walk in the park.

He reached for his stash of antacid tablets and popped one into his mouth. Dinner together a couple times a week didn't cut it—for him either.

He hitched his Armani suit's left sleeve and consulted his watch. 7:35 A.M. He stabbed "Lobby" again and dragged his focus to the first of his many meetings.

Callie Evans perched her designer frames atop her hundred-dollar haircut and pulled her attention from her computer screen. "Hey, boss. How did you make out? Should I be calling Legal?"

"Not yet, Callie," Ethan said warmly to his assistant. "Just one minor complication to work through before the island is ours." *That is, if you could call Lily Greensly and her formidable passion for everything connected to Loon Lake and her family, minor.* "It's a game of finesse, Callie."

"Oh, you'll seal the deal. You always do."

"Sure I will. But in the meantime, set something up at Mamma Mia's, please. Friday night. Early, around six."

"Oh, Emma must be excited. Tell her to have an extra dessert for me." Callie patted her flat belly. "There are more calories in Mamma's cheesecake than I eat in a year."

Ethan flashed a smile toward his flamboyant assistant and strode through the doorway into one the most coveted corner offices on Bay Street.

His steps slowed for a second as his gaze fell on the stack of files centered neatly on his desk and the row of sticky notes covering the top half of his computer screen. This is the price I pay for staying out of the office an extra day, he thought, grimacing at the paperwork, but getting Osprey Island was priority-one right now.

He allowed his gaze to travel to the gleaming glass behind his desk and the view of Toronto's harbor. Morning mist still circled the upper stories of the adjacent office buildings. Beyond, a dark and serious Lake Ontario buffeted the shoreline, leaving a sticky line of foam each time it receded. Farther out, a tanker plowed through the white caps, its plume of black smoke swept into the downtown area by an offshore breeze.

Lily would certainly have something to say about the state of this lake, he thought. She'd actually *do* something. He eyed a stack of environmental reading material he'd been obligated to study before breaking ground at Loon Lake. Was the answer buried somewhere in that massive pile of printed material?

Deciding to deal with more easily solved problems, he settled into the leather chair and stretched for his stack of messages. He quickly scanned the notes, only pausing when he came to the final message.

Jim Murdock, the manager of his Toronto hotel, was tied up with an automaker's conference and wouldn't make this morning's meeting.

Ethan tipped his chair back and swung his feet to his desk top. Jim was a bit like himself, Ethan acknowledged. A detail man. Ambitious. Hates to miss a critical meeting. I bet he'd appreciate an update after hours. Ethan's feet hit the floor as his hand reached for the phone.

"Jim. Ethan here," he said to Jim's answering machine. "No problem about missing the meeting.

I'll drop by the hotel tonight and bring you up to speed."

Last night Lily had politely turned down his awkward offer of a private plane ride to the city; she'd take the train. But citing the diminishing grant funds, she'd graciously and, on the behalf of the university, accepted a free pass to the downtown Weatherall Hotel.

If he just happened to run into Lily, well . . .

Lily scanned the downtown hotel's Mediterranean Room with manufactured nonchalance and smoothed a hand over the back of her dress. Assured her cotton floral skirt swung freely, she stepped across the threshold and sunk into carpet as deep as the peat in Blackbird Swamp. Feeling as if she had walked onto the movie set of a 1940s film, she scanned the crowd of diners for a table.

Textured wallpaper the color of a Starbucks latte set off the darker hue of the wainscoting. Chandeliers, pieces of twisted wrought iron and glass filled the room with romantic ambience. The hotel's brochure claimed the legendary Mediterranean Room to be the site of more marriage proposals than any other restaurant in Canada.

Couples populated the room, holding hands across pristine damask tablecloths, laughing quietly over shared intimacies.

Her urge to celebrate, city-style, was diminishing rapidly. *Why didn't I just order room service?*

She inched backward, planning her retreat, when the maître d' spied her and expressed mock horror that a woman of her beauty need dine alone.

"I want a table somewhere private," she whispered to his tuxedo-clad back as they navigated the tables.

"Of course, my dear. I understand. But how will eligible gentlemen find you if I hide you in the corner?"

"I prefer to be alone."

"Ah, nursing a broken heart, my dear?"

What, is there a sign on my back?

"Thank you," she said, ignoring his comment, and settled into the plush corner bench.

Her table overlooked a garden of exotic ferns and manicured evergreens. Tiny twinkle lights circled the garden's lush perimeter.

Now this is worth braving the crowd of twosomes for, she decided. *And after all, I deserve a special dinner*, she reminded herself. Professor Nesbitt's Finance Committee had given her the go-ahead for her next project earlier today. All she had to do was fund-raise the remaining fifty percent and Loon Lake would be the site for another comprehensive study.

She couldn't stop a smile. And to top it off, a

night in Toronto's ritziest hotel. After refusing his initial grandiose gesture, it had been relatively easy to accept Ethan's stay-for-free coupons.

"So, I take it by the look on your face your day was successful," a deep voice boomed from behind a potted fern.

Lily jumped. It was him. Already she knew the voice. Rich, mellow and . . . sexy.

"Mr. Weatherall . . . er, Ethan."

He wore a serious navy suit and a crisp white shirt. His tie was loosened at the neck. A swirl of light brown chest hair peeked out from the V of his collar. Probably the most formally dressed man in the room and so handsome her throat hurt when she tried to swallow.

He eyed the empty spot next to her and raised his eyebrows. "May I?"

"It's your place." She softened the phrase with a generous wave. "Have you eaten?"

"Yes. Earlier. But if you don't mind, I'll join you for a coffee."

Lily found herself wondering with whom he'd shared his meal.

"I dropped by for a meeting with my hotel manager and thought I'd swing through the dining room. You know, to see who's out and about."

"And? Is there anybody of note, anybody

famous?" Lily scanned the room, excited by the notion she might see a celebrity.

"Kind of quiet tonight. Except for the deputy mayor over there by the dessert cart and the star of the Stratford Festival's latest production." He nodded his head to the left. "There. With the red dress."

Lily turned, anxious to catch a glimpse of a Canadian superstar. A white light flashed, and she raised her hands to her burning eyes.

"Sorry, miss. Do you mind, Mr. Weatherall? I'm short for tomorrow's paper. Could you share your date's name, please?"

Date? Ethan and I? Together? She opened her fingers a crack. A young man cradling an enormous camera and flashing a press card stood beside the table. Dots of blue light danced in front of her face and she pressed her fingertips to her pupils.

"Close your eyes for a few seconds and it goes away." His breath moved across the top her head, and she knew he must be leaning across the small table. His hand patted her forearm consolingly.

"This is Lily Greensly, from Loon Lake." Ethan directed to the reporter. "She's in the city today presenting to the university's marine research team."

She straightened in the chair and smiled toward

the reporter, pleased Ethan had remembered the details of her visit.

The reporter's eyebrows lifted at the Loon Lake reference.

Excitement coursed through Lily's body. First a promise of funding and now a mention in the paper. Media exposure for her cause!

Ethan smiled into the camera and continued speaking. "Loon Lake, of course, is the home of my flagship hotel the Nirvana, the first in my new hotel chain."

The reporter scribbled hastily onto a notepad, and Lily sunk into the cushioned back of her chair. Of course he was promoting his gazillion-dollar investment, not her push to prevent corruption of the lake's resources.

Ethan's words blurred into background buzz as she forced herself to consider the menu choices. The fish sounded tasty, but the chicken, on the other hand . . .

"Lily." Ethan's voice cut into her thoughts. "Have you a comment for this gentleman?"

"Me?" She stared into the reporter's face, searching for a starting-off place. "Um . . . yes," she said, wishing her voice didn't sound so shaky.

"My family's lodge and the Nirvana depend on the water quality of Loon Lake and ultimately the survival of the fish living there."

Surprise registered in the reporter's eyes followed by an admiring glance. His pen raced across the page. He probably thinks I'm somebody, Lily presumed. Thanks to Ethan.

"I'm hopeful Mr. Weatherall will join with me and the Friends of Loon Lake to ensure the lake's healthy existence."

Ethan nodded a visual "touché" across the table.

"The research group I work with is open to support, financially and in spirit," Lily finished strongly, while scrambling in her purse for Professor Nesbitt's card.

The reporter pocketed the card and moved off.

"Well done," Ethan said, admiration reflecting in his eyes. "I hope something comes of it. The city's movers and shakers read that guy's column, believe it or not."

"Thank you. I mean really, I could never hope for that kind of exposure on my own."

"My pleasure." His gaze moved over her face, resting when it found her eyes.

His broad smile was replaced with a more intense, questioning look and she wondered, had he come here hoping to find her? Her heart skipped a beat and she raised the menu to cover her face, suddenly shy.

He's completely wrong for me. We live in worlds as different as night and day. Plus, she wasn't ready to give her heart away again. Especially to someone who might damage, or at the very least exploit, the very thing she was working to protect.

Deciding to blame her attraction to Ethan on the Mediterranean Room's romantic charm, Lily looked up into the told-you-so smile of the hovering maître d'.

The distance from the dining room to the bank of elevators was entirely too short, Lily decided, as they neared a pair of stainless steel doors.

She'd eaten an entire plate of chicken alfredo without tasting a single bite, while Ethan had drank several cups of black coffee. He'd explained the history of his cosmopolitan hotel, and she'd found herself fascinated with the intriguing past of the gorgeous old building.

"Tenth floor, please," she responded to his inquiring glance. Ethan's arm brushed against hers as he tapped a series of buttons and she smiled, realizing he intended to escort her to right to her room and she'd have a few minutes more of his pleasant company. She ignored the little voice, warning her to execute caution in the presence of this gorgeous man. She was a grown woman, she told herself sternly. Plenty old enough to enjoy a man's company without losing perspective—or her heart.

The elevator doors closed smoothly and they were swept upward. Haunting strains of a Mozart concerto filled the elevator, making Lily almost wish her room was on the twenty-fifth floor.

The doors slid open and his hand cupped her elbow as they exited the elevator. Without hesitation he chose a hallway leading to the right. "You said room 1032, right?

"Do you know all your hotels this well?"

"No way, but I cut my teeth on this one. Played in these hallways when I was a kid. Our nanny, Miss Scott, used to bring us down here for dinner with my father. Pretty much the only way we'd ever get a chance to see him."

He sounded matter-of-fact, as if an absent father was the norm. Where had his mother been?

She pulled her key card from her pocket as they approached her door. *Should I ask him in?* "Thank you again for the room," Lily said. "Saves my research budget for more useful things like software programs and lab equipment."

"Glad to help the cause." Ethan didn't move. "Gives me a chance to thank you for the fish fry. Your parents are great," he added more soberly. "Made me feel welcome."

He reached for her hands and folded them into his own and her heart did a flip-flop. "Well, it's been"—he paused and placed a finger under her chin, tilting her face until her gaze met with his— "fun. You're like no woman in this city, Lily."

There he goes again, saying my name at the end of his sentence. The soft inflection he dropped drew her in, created an intimate moment out of an ordinary one.

He cradled her elbow in his hand and gently propelled her closer to him as the cleaning staff rolled a huge stainless steel cart by.

Somewhere on their floor, muffled voices voiced good-nights and a door closed.

His face breezed by her cheek as he reached for her card. "May I?" His familiar concoction of musk and mint ignited her senses. Whether a designer cologne or just toothpaste and aftershave, its effect was insanely seductive.

He needed a shave, she observed. The slope of his cheek, pebbled with stubble, although unusual for him, was not a bad look, really, she decided.

Her feet apparently had a mind of their own, and she remained frozen to the spot as he reached around her body and sliced the card through the slot.

"Darn." The plastic card tumbled from his fingers and landed at their feet. "Sorry, I'm all thumbs," Ethan said, bending to retrieve the card.

The strip of tanned skin revealed between the pristine white of his shirt collar and the neat barber's line of his thick black hair flushed red.

He's flustered, she realized with surprise and a

smidgen of pleasure. She discreetly stepped back from the door.

Key in hand, he turned to face her, grinning. "One more try and you're in, I promise."

The door clicked open with his next attempt and he stepped aside, gallantly waving her inside. Turning to face him, she suddenly felt as if she was on a first date, silly expectations included. Would he call her? He certainly knew where to find her. He reached out and caught up her hand in his. Oh my. Would he kiss her? Did she want him too? She looked up into his face and he brought his other hand to cover hers. He dropped his gaze to the floor before returning to meet her eyes.

Taking a half step forward, Ethan was now disturbingly close. Her pulse quickened and she swallowed hard. It's okay if he kisses me, she rationalized. Adults do that sometimes. Doesn't have to be a big deal.

Lost in his chocolate-sweet eyes she let out a soft breath. He definitely was going to kiss her. His head dipped slightly and his lips dropped a warm kiss to her cheek.

Well, she wasn't wrong about the kiss, just its destination. When relief trumped disappointment, she realized that she wasn't ready for a man to kiss her again, anyway.

"Great to have run into you, Lily," he said. "Just call down to the front desk if you need anything at all. I'm glad to do my bit for the lake and your project." He smiled with the friendly words and clasped both her hands in his.

"Thank you, Ethan. You've been more than generous." With nothing else to say and in light of the awkward situation, she waited for her hands back. Silence yawned between them. A siren wailed somewhere in the city. Certain he must feel the clamminess of her palms still locked in his grasp, she gently unfurled her fingers. "Well, I guess I'll say good night then," she said.

He glanced down at their locked hands and dropped them, as if he hadn't realized they were still connected.

"Sure. But there are some documents I intended to courier out to you tomorrow that I'll give to you tonight. He extracted a sheaf of papers from his inner breast pocket and handed them to her. "Have a look at these tonight, please, and let me know what you think. The Hideaway is a special place, loaded with tradition and memories, and it would be a shame for all that to end with your generation. I hope this information helps alleviate some of your family's concerns."

The shift in topic caught her off guard. The

Hideaway? She glanced at the papers in her hand, confusion clouding her thoughts.

"Good night, then. I'll talk you again, at the lake, I presume," she said as she edged the suite's door closed.

After sliding the bolt into place, she settled at the elegant writing desk and plucked the heavy bond sheets from the envelope.

Boldface lettering headed the legal-looking document. **OFFER TO PURCHASE**. What did he want to purchase?

Unwilling to plow through the legal jargon, she scanned the paragraphs. From the jumble of jargon, familiar words leaped from the page. "The property registered to Lily Greensly and hereby designated as Osprey Island." Her hands began to shake. He wanted her property?

Recollections of dinner, his smile as he spoke from across the candlelit table, the almost-kiss swirled in her head.

The antique chair toppled backward to the floor as she rose swiftly to her feet. Forcing air deep into her lungs, she picked up the paper again. Slowly and deliberately she stilled her shaking hand and focused on the dancing typeface.

Chapter Five

Lily lifted her hand to her cheek. It burned hot under her trembling fingers. Was the accidental meeting in the restaurant meant to worm his way into her good books? Pave the way for . . . this? She fanned the sheets across her face as a second flood of heat scorched her face. Her legs felt like rubber, and her arm flailed behind her for the toppled chair.

What did he want with Osprey Island anyway? What did it have to do with the Nirvana or, for that matter, the Hideaway? she wondered, remembering his comments about the Hideaway's traditions. Goose bumps torpedoed from her fingertips to her shoulders. She perched on the edge of the seat and once again smoothed the creased papers. *Calm down,* she directed herself. *Breathe. Read it slowly.*

A thick business card, embossed with the Weatherall logo and a list of Ethan's private numbers was clipped to the first sheet. Snapping the card to the desk, her eyes went on to devour the details of the document.

Apparently the Weatheralls wanted her island for use as a helipad. The sum mentioned was far beyond its appraised value. About three times as much.

Lily's glance darted from wall to tabletop to the entertainment center. In the top corner, left of the big screen television she found the time. Red digital numbers flashed 10:15 P.M.

She leaped to her feet and snatched the phone from its cradle. If Ethan Weatherall thought she was a country bumpkin who'd swoon at his feet, pen in hand, well . . . he was about to find out differently!

The hotel's phone base was faced with a row of tiny lights and miniscule type. Lily gritted her teeth and bent to decipher the fine print before choosing an option. Glancing at his card, she stabbed in his residence number.

Bravado seeped from her rigid form with every ring. Maybe he wasn't home yet? She was certain he'd said he lived only a couple of blocks from the hotel. Maybe he went out somewhere after he left the hotel? She chewed on her lower lip.

Five rings. Maybe he went to a club? A club crowded with Toronto's movers and shakers, the kind of people that drank designer cocktails and nibbled crab cakes. She groaned softly as she imagined the newspaper reporter snapping a second shot of the city's favorite man-about-town. Only this photo would show him coupled with a sophisticated woman, her chin tilted upward, laughing knowingly at his remarks.

Lily sank into the bed's downy coverlet and clicked off the phone.

The faux-Moroccan ceiling tiles blurred as she stared upward. *Why am I so blind when it comes to men?* Doug couldn't commit to a woman who might become a burden, and apparently to Ethan she was merely a means to an end.

Her fingers went to her cheek and the place where he'd smoothed a soft kiss. When she'd looked into his eyes hadn't she seen her own vulnerability mirrored back? She burrowed into the pillows.

Tears slid from the corners of her eyes, pooling onto the coverlet. Lily swiped at her eyes and shifted from the wet spot. Through the bathroom doorway she spied a box of tissue placed next to a huge whirlpool tub.

Snatching the complimentary robe from its hook, she plucked a bath product from the selection of tiny glass bottles. Soon steam, scented with lavender, billowed from the tub.

Water lapped against her chin and slowly her legs stretched to fill the length of the tub. She tipped her head back until it rested against the tile.

Tomorrow, she'd visit Delaney's shop. Her best friend had been at her side through the dog days of the broken engagement and had become an expert at serving up just the right amount of vicarious indignation, peppered with her cutting sense of humor.

Lily slid deeper into the silky water. If I had even half of Delaney's in-your-face approach to life, Lily thought, Ethan's big real estate deal would be dead in the water already.

Chapter Six

Ethan had covered the few blocks from the hotel to his condo in long strides without noticing the concrete high-rises that lined the street or hearing the hum of late-night traffic. Hands stuffed in pockets, head down, he walked by his doorman and into the elevator. Lily and his misplaced kiss were all he could think about. He'd wanted to kiss her so badly, but he needed to get this whole island deal behind them so there would no blurring of lines. He would hate for Lily to think he was trying to influence her decision. Fact was, he wanted to kiss her whether she agreed to the sale or not.

Ethan nudged Emma's door open and slipped silently into her room. In the pink glow cast from her bedside lamp, his sister slept soundly. Her face, free of any worry lines, belied her age, and looked almost cherubic in the soft light. Kind of like the chubby little angels on the cover of her favorite book, he thought as he stood in the peaceful room.

Checking in on his twin sister was a habit formed in the months after their mother left. He'd slept better back then, knowing she'd slept safely, her arms laced through a tumble of pillows, surrounded by Clarence and her other stuffed animals.

Here in Emma's world, *his* life made sense. Had real purpose. Her world was measured and predictable. His, well . . .

Ethan tipped his head back and sighed audibly, remembering a day chocked full with hurried meetings and an unforgiving timetable. But it was the only life he knew and he was good at it. Real good. The rush of maneuvering an innovative concept through the channels of paperwork and watching the business grow to international proportions was intoxicating. But exhausting. He raked his fingers through his hair as if to rid himself of thoughts of Weatherall Enterprises.

A sliver of moon rising over the condos near the lake caught his eye. A smile pulled at his mouth. Was Lily looking at the same moon?

He glanced at Emma's sleeping form again, wanting to tell her about his last couple of days. Her even breaths stirred Emma's form only slightly. He turned and walked quietly toward the door.

"Big E," a sleep-laden voice called out. "Come back. Tell me something."

It was a game they'd played whenever Ethan came home from work. Emma would insist he tell her something, anything, about his day. Whether it was a story about the broken vending machine in the coffee room, his doubts about a flagging mutual fund he'd bought on speculation, or even a description of Callie's latest crazy hairstyle, Emma enjoyed them equally. When satisfied she'd heard enough about Ethan's day, she would then share hers.

"Emma, I'm sorry. Didn't want to wake you. Just checking in." Ethan hesitated for a second. Sorry he'd disturbed his sister, but happy they'd connected after all.

"It's okay." Emma shifted higher until she rested in a sea of plump pillows. She patted the edge of the bed and pleaded with her sleep-heavy eyes. "Just one little story."

Ethan smiled and pushed into the pile of much-mended teddy bears. "All right, then." He cleared his throat loudly for effect and mentally scanned for the most significant event.

"I met a pretty woman named Lily," he began, "and she lives in a log home on the shores of Loon Lake and she loves to fish." His words fell easily into the dim room, pleasant and predictable, like a fairy tale.

"Wow. Really, Big E?"

"Really. But she has another job too. She takes care of the lake, so people won't ruin it."

Excitement heightened her tone. "She sounds like a good lady. Can she come here someday?" Emma pulled free of the comforter and clapped her hands.

"Actually, she's here now. At our hotel."

He pictured Lily settling into the gold and white suite. Maybe phoning her father to discuss his offer for Osprey Island or maybe going over the notes from her meeting earlier in the day.

"But she goes back to Loon Lake tomorrow. This isn't her kind of place." His lighthearted words slowed as he neared the end of his sentence and he realized how apt his words really were. By tomorrow afternoon she'd be rounding Greensly Bay, her hair flying in the wind.

Could his overly generous offer sway a woman so committed to family and tradition? He remembered the ancient snapshot of Grandpa Greensly centered in the Hideaway's hallway and his gut told him it wasn't likely. Even with the aging Hideaway in need of a cash injection, Lily would hate to sell the island he needed to meet his father's stringent conditions and finish the project he'd devoted his life to for the last eighteen months. He dropped his head back and stared unseeingly at the ceiling. So much for a happy ending to this particular story.

If a childhood full of boarding schools and separations from Emma had taught him anything, it was that happy endings belonged only in books. Certainly his parent's ill-fated marriage hadn't done anything to change that opinion.

He pulled himself heavily from the bed. "Back to sleep, okay," he said briskly, noting her drooping eyes. "How about I hear your story in the morning over breakfast? I bet we could convince Miss Scott to make us waffles with syrup and bananas." The doting Miss Scott liked nothing better than feeding her two favorite people and didn't get the chance nearly as often as she liked.

Sidetracked, Emma nodded emphatically and cocooned into her comforter. "G'night, Big E."

The phone purred from the living room.

"Wait, Ethan," Emma beckoned him closer. "Miss Scott says you're going back to Loon Lake soon. Why don't you take Lily something nice from the city? So she'll like it more."

He patted Emma's shoulder affectionately. "Good idea, Em. Now get some rest."

What would make Lily like city life? She wasn't into designer clothes or jewelry. Cash for her research project maybe, he thought ruefully, as he padded down the hallway toward the ringing phone. Weatherall Enterprises routinely supported non-profit groups.

His steps slowed as he considered the options. He stopped and stared into the darkness. Would she accept help from him now? Or would it look too much like a bribe? His shoulders dropped with the weight of the hour and the problem.

He had the connections. . . . He could leave Weatherall off the list. *That's it.* His feet moved forward on the strength of the decision. A few introductions to the right people were really all she needed. Lily was a passionate speaker for her cause, she could take it from there.

The phone stopped ringing as he strode into his home office and clicked on the computer. Hunched over the glowing screen, Ethan monitored the names and addresses of Toronto's business elite as the electronic pages scrolled past.

Carefully, he weeded out his father's cronies, men who ate neophytes like Lily for breakfast. He slowed the screen as potential investors presented themselves. His cursor hovered on the name of a dot-com success story; Mark Roscoe—young, successful, and according to Callie, hugely attractive to woman everywhere. He stared at the man's name, mulling over what he knew of Roscoe. He pictured Mark and Lily together, Lily's maps and graphs spread across an intimate table for two. Mark would marvel at her passion and sign on as a benefactor to her cause, winning Lily's respect forever.

He jabbed and held the double arrow down key to advance the screen and watched as the data on Roscoe Enterprises blurred in a warp-speed advance toward the next potential financier. There were lots of others, no reason to jump at the first one.

Ethan leaned into the screen as the information on the Calgary-based Southerland Group appeared. Now here was something. Solid company, credible history, middle-aged, married CEO . . .

Chapter Seven

The sign in Delaney's hair salon and art gallery window was flipped to the Closed side. Held captive in the black and chrome barber's chair, Lily was beginning to regret her decision to let Delaney trim her hair.

"Ouch."

"Sorry, Lily. But really, your hair's a mess." Delaney Forbes stretched Lily's tangled blond curls through the comb. "Why don't you let me cut it shorter? You could do short. Wispy little bangs maybe?" She piled Lily's hair on top of her head. "A few streaks?"

She should have known Delaney would push for a more drastic change. They'd had a version of

75

this conversation too many times to count. "No way. I know it's a disaster. But I like my hair. I love the wind blowing through it when I'm on the lake. Makes me feel free."

"Free of any kind of style," Delaney muttered through gritted teeth as she worked detangling solution into her best friend's hair. "Now that needs to soak in for a few minutes," she said, and spun the chair to face the window and Buttermilk Falls' main street.

"Thanks for taking me without an appointment, Delaney," Lily said. They watched a minivan struggle to park in front of the Laundromat. "I knew you'd make me feel better."

"That's what I'm here for, girlfriend. Besides, it's a slow week."

And that's what Lily loved the most about Delaney. She held back nothing, pulled no punches. She'd listened attentively to Lily's story about Ethan, the kiss-that-went-astray, and the deal he'd tried to pull.

"So, the way I see it, Lily, is that Ethan is genuinely interested in you. And, hair issues aside"— Delaney smiled sweetly—"who could blame him?" She turned Lily's chair back to the mirror and with a game-show-host wave, deemed her gorgeous. "Or, he's overdosed on his own testosterone and trampling little people is just another day's work."

Lily shook her head at Delaney's remark and quickly leaped to defend his character. "No," she interjected, "there's a human being lurking under the Armani suit, somewhere."

Delaney rolled her eyes. "So just so I'm clear. You're not mad at him anymore?"

"Well, no. Not really. I don't know him well enough to be certain if he was up to something or not. But I believe you can tell a lot about a person by their eyes. And I liked what I saw behind his when we were talking."

"Those were dollar signs, sister."

"I saw a glimpse of humanity while we were in the boat too," Lily continued, ignoring Delaney's aside. "He was genuinely excited about the opening of the Nirvana."

"Who wouldn't get exited about making more millions, Lily?"

"So what do I do? He's coming back for the Friends of Loon Lake meeting tomorrow night."

Delaney narrowed her skillfully made-up eyes and tapped a lacquered nail against her chin. "Do nothing. Be cool. You e-mailed your refusal to sell the island, right?"

"Right. In a boldface, one-inch font."

"So he knows you won't sell. So here's the thing: If he asks you out or makes a move, then I'd say he likes you—not just your island.

If he gives you the brush off . . . well, there's your answer." Delaney began fiddling with the arrangement of framed prints covering the back wall of the shop, effectively ending the conversation and switching from an advisory to a shopkeeping mode.

Lily considered Delaney's statement. If it only was that simple. She chewed her bottom lip.

The bell over the shop tinkled, heralding Tommy Sands and the arrival of the *Toronto Star*.

"There you go, Delaney." Buttermilk Falls' local reporter acknowledged both women with a shy smile. "Better have a look at page seventeen. Social page is pretty interesting today. Already sold more of these papers today than the Buttermilk Falls *Herald*."

Delaney grabbed the newspaper and thumbed quickly to the society column.

"Lily, it's you! You're in the paper!" Delaney's gaze remained fastened on the page as she continued to speak. "What's this?" She pushed her nose deeper into the paper. "Urban legend, Ethan Weatherall, was spotted canoodling with one fresh-from-the-farm Lily Greensly. If it's true that opposites attract, then this mismatch just might work."

Lily leaped from the chair. "Give me that." She snapped the paper open, her gaze immediately drawn to the photo at the bottom of the page. "Why can't I ever look decent in a picture?"

"It's not so bad," Delaney said, her voice lacking conviction. "You look . . . young."

"I look awestruck, like a teenager out on the town for the first time. It's not fair, Delaney. After all, I lived in Toronto for four years.

"True."

"Okay, I admit, I hardly left the biology labs, but still. . . . Oh, who am I kidding Delaney, I may have just as well got my degree by correspondence for all the socializing I did."

She continued to scan the article, searching for a reference to the University's marine research program. Dripping with innuendo, the reporter had managed to link the grand opening of the Nirvana with her work, followed with a brief mention of Professor Nesbitt's program and his goal of protecting Ontario's inland fisheries.

Lily let out a breath. A mention in a national paper certainly would raise the program's profile. The reporter's humiliating farm-girl jibe might be worth it if Dr. Nesbitt received even one donation from the paper's coverage.

"Delaney! Get this goop out of my hair. I need to go home and call Professor Nesbitt." She slid forward in the chair and began fumbling with the strings of the plastic cape Delaney had draped over her T-shirt.

"Hold on, missy. Are you going to take this lying down?" Delaney flapped the society page in Lily's face. "That reporter practically called you a hick."

Delaney scrunched down and positioned her sleek black bob next to her friend's long, tangled tresses. "Come on, Lily." She fingered a section of dripping strands with obvious anticipation. "Give me an hour and I'll make you as sophisticated as any of these city gals," she wheedled, pointing to a photo taken at the opening of a swanky bar in Toronto's entertainment district.

"But I don't want to look like . . . that." Lily grimaced at the picture of a lanky model type with an asymmetrical bob swinging provocatively across one eye.

"Trust me. A good stylist knows her client's lifestyle. I'd create a look even you could manage."

Delaney cringed at Lily's disparaging look. "I mean with your early mornings and limited styling skills you need something simple and fresh, but sexy and fun.

Maybe she's right, Lily thought as Delaney began rifling through a stack of industry magazines. *I've been wearing my hair this way since I was fourteen.*

Doug had admired her youthful look. She rubbed the pale band of skin where her engagement ring had been. He'd said he wanted to spend the rest of his life with her too.

She glanced again at the society page. Why couldn't they take her seriously? A sobering thought raised its ugly head. Would it be easier to raise funds if she looked more professional?

Would Ethan have felt more comfortable presenting his offer earlier in the evening if he'd considered her an equal partner when it came to business? Could the humiliating end to their evening have been prevented with a better haircut?

It was definitely time to move on. Make a change. "Delaney?" Her voice rang louder than she intended.

"Yes, Lily." Delaney stood frozen, the latest issue of *Head Style* magazine clutched to her chest.

"Promise you won't make me regret this."

"You have my word," Delaney said solemnly and reached eagerly for a clump of blond curls. "Just tell me you're doing this for yourself. Not for me or Ethan Weatherall."

Lily twisted a strand of hair around her finger and considered her answer. Up until a few days ago it might have been for somebody else. But she was tired of hiding from the world. She was bright and sexy and fun and it was time everyone knew it.

Hey, maybe pain does make you stronger. "Do your thing, Delaney Forbes."

Ethan put his shoulder to the library's glass door and shoved it open. His long strides took him toward the buzz of conversation and the aroma of a fresh pot of coffee.

Would Lily be here? He knew outsiders generally fared badly in a room full of locals. Even if she was mad at him, at least she'd be a familiar face. His pulse quickened as he recalled the softness of her tumbling curls and how sweet her hair smelled. And the kiss. The small, sweet kiss had brightened his spirits. The sky looked bluer today, the grass greener.

Clichés are clichés for a reason, he decided— she *was* like a breath of fresh country air in his stale city life.

His hand slid to the breast pocket of his jacket and he fingered the e-mail he had received from Lily. The giant refusal. He'd spilled his coffee on his shirt when Callie had showed him the printout. No negotiation, no thanks for the offer. Just no.

Part of the game, he valiantly tried to convince himself. A negotiation tactic, maybe? No, probably not. But the facts remained the same: the Greenslys needed cash to keep the Hideaway afloat. Surely, after more consideration and the chance to talk it over with her parents, she'd change her mind. He rubbed his chin in frustration. He wasn't accustomed to negotiating with a woman.

Suddenly it hit him. He slammed his open palm to his forehead. Men kept business and personal separate. But woman didn't so much. They dragged emotion and feelings into everything. Even though he'd tried to handle the situation with sensitivity, Lily probably thought he'd sought her out at the hotel on purpose. Of course, he had, but not because of Osprey Island.

Relief soared through his body. He'd just make a point never to mention the island unless they were sitting on opposite sides of a conference table.

The noise from the room grew louder and his gaze settled on a hastily penned note taped to the side of a coffee can perched on top of a stack of chairs. It politely solicited donations to the Friends of Loon Lake fund. He plucked his wallet from the back pocket of his Levi's and fingered the thick layer of cash. Twenty? He considered the crowd. Too much? Not enough?

He stood on his toes and leaned in, closing one eye as his face neared the can. Bills? With his free hand he tilted the can toward the light. The clatter of loonies against the thin tin ricocheted down the hallway. He pressed closer to the chairs. Yes . . .

No wait . . . Yes. A couple of twenties and a few fives lay among the coins. He let his weight fall to his heels, satisfied he'd averted a blunder. People hated to be made to look cheap.

"Looking for change, Ethan?" Her tone was cool, polite.

He spun to face her, a crisp twenty poking through his fingers. "Er, no." He jammed the bill through the slot and smiled. Some things are better ignored than acknowledged. And after her curt e-mail message, he was relieved she was still speaking to him.

They stood too close for comfort, his size tens toe-to-toe with her pointy brown leather boots. His gaze followed the supple leather clinging to her curvy calves and he swallowed a lump the size of a Tim Hortons muffin.

"The meeting is about to start. We better go in."

His gaze traveled up from the boots to a camel colored skirt that swung just above her knees. Her sweater was the same color of blue as her eyes. A delicate silver necklace sparkled prettily in the v-shaped neckline, its heart pendant nestled in the hollow of her neck.

But something else was different. Her hair? Shorter maybe? Shades of blond flowed into one another every time her head moved. Layers of varying length, the longest just skimming her shoulders had tamed her free-flowing look. He couldn't tear his eyes away. If anything, she was prettier than he remembered.

"Before we go in, Lily, I wanted to apologize for the inappropriate timing of my offer to purchase the island. That was a business matter, better left for office hours."

Her tight-lipped cordiality softened slightly with her reply. "Apology accepted. But the answer is still no."

He nodded acknowledgment. No surprise there. And there would be other opportunities for him to make his business pitch. Just not tonight.

He followed her into a roomful of strangers, most of whom seemed intent on watching the newcomer and the town's favorite daughter find a seat.

In a single movement, he placed his hands on the metal backs of the two remaining chairs and pulled them back from the table. The clanging of the entangled chair legs brought the remaining few uninterested folk over to the masses.

A large woman outfitted in a grape-colored outfit and seated directly across the oval conference table nudged her neighbor and whispered, "He looks older than his picture, don't you think?"

Ignoring her table mate's comment, a bird-sized woman, whom Ethan remembered as Merv-from-Cabin-One's wife, flashed Ethan a conspiratorial smile. "So wonderful to see you again, Mr. Weatherall. I do hope you enjoyed the Greenslys' barbecue as much as I did."

"I certainly did, Edith. They don't make food like that up in Toronto." The elderly woman preened her salt-and-pepper hair with her thin fingers.

"Merv have any luck catching the big one after I left?"

"Not yet, Mr. Weatherall. But he's a determined man. He'll bring it in before the summer is over."

Ethan settled back and scanned the group, deciding it didn't really matter much where a meeting was held, city or country. People are people.

He turned to Lily. Annoyance was written all over her face. Now what had he done? Under his scrutiny, her expression quickly changed to a bland smile. Didn't she want the Nirvana to succeed? Or was it just him she didn't like?

The large lady in purple cleared her throat and proclaimed the meeting in progress. They worked their way through correspondence, reports, building code updates, and environmental information that pertained to Loon Lake.

They really know what they're doing, Ethan thought, impressed with their thoroughness. He knew his team had followed the municipal guidelines for development on the lake, so he wasn't worried about a surprise attack. There had been an inspector on-site weekly for the last eighteen months.

"Now it's time for the fund-raising report," someone announced. "Lily, please bring the committee up to speed."

Lily slid her chair back and stood, a thick sheaf of papers clutched in her hand. "As most of you know Loon Lake has been the lucky recipient of the University of Toronto's research grant." A spatter of applause filled the room. Lily blushed prettily and continued, "Under Professor Nesbitt's guidance, I'll be able to complete my study of the indigenous fishes, the water quality, and the effect of development on our lake."

A nodding of heads around the oval table indicated satisfaction with Lily and her work.

"Lucky for us, while in Toronto, I received a portion of the additional funding needed from the university."

"Oh, we know about your trip to Toronto," Edith tittered, her inference to the society-page photo precipitating a round of approving smiles directed toward Ethan.

Lily dipped her chin and continued. "I'm pleased to announce they'll provide fifty percent of the monies required.

She raised her head to acknowledge the second spontaneous patter of applause. Ethan joined the crowd in enthusiastic appreciation. *Man, she looks sweet when she blushes.*

"Hold on, everyone." Lily tucked a smooth blond lock behind one ear. "Fifty percent is good, but we need to fund-raise the rest."

Heavy sighs and a low grumbling began, picking up momentum as the committee members debated the merits of bake sales and raffles.

Lily surveyed the crowd. "I know, I know. I feel the same. It's hard work, but I'm sure we all agree about one thing." The crowd quieted. "Loon Lake is in jeopardy if we don't do this." A murmur of assent rippled through the crowd. "In fact, all the freshwater lakes in the province are in jeopardy if groups like ours don't pay attention." Lily's voice became stronger and two pink spots glowed high on her cheeks. "We can do it. Fund-raising Committee, let's hear some ideas!" She scanned the faces of her audience expectantly before plunking back to her seat.

Ethan drummed his fingers on the tabletop, hesitant to jump into the conversation. He'd never even been to a yard sale. He reached to the reports piled in the center of the table and pretended to scrutinize the data and waited for Lily's next move.

Should he tell her about the Southerland Group? Or would she think he was ingratiating himself in front of her friends? He couldn't afford to annoy her any more.

For the moment he'd just listen in on the fund-raising ideas and bide his time. He would tell Lily about the Southerland Group later, in private. Maybe after the meeting? Let it be her work, her connections that brought in the cash flow, not his. He would just drop a name, no more.

The room began to buzz with conversation as the crowd split into small groups. He quietly inched his chair back and worked his way through the milling bodies circling the coffee urn.

He sipped the thin brew and rubbed his eyes. It had been a long day. The short flight out to Loon Lake had been a reprieve. The tension in his back had eased with the fading of the city lights. As the countryside had become less populated, the terrain dark and rugged, a peacefulness settled over him. He looked forward to spending the night in his private suite in the still-unoccupied Nirvana. He intended to be up in time to check out the sunrise Lily had assured him his guests would love.

"Okay, that's it, then. We will have a dance to raise money. Please note the motion." The large lady in purple boomed the consensus toward the scribbling secretary. "We will hold the event in two weeks' time. With an aquatic theme and a midnight buffet, it's sure to attract a lot of couples." She smiled radiantly for the crowd before adding in a more matter-of-fact tone, "And with really nothing else going on around here, we're bound to bring in a pile of dough. Meeting adjourned."

Ethan had been curiously quiet throughout the meeting, Lily noted. So far she'd been unable to determine if she was being ignored, which would mean Delaney's prediction that he was only interested in the island was accurate. Or was he genuinely interested in the lake's future and intent on processing all the information?

Either way the meeting was adjourned, and the room was emptying fast. She took a deep breath and forced her feet to move in his direction. There was only one way to find out.

"I'm impressed. You flew all the way in from Toronto for our meeting?"

Ethan's smile relaxed her somewhat.

"I hope it was worth it," she continued. "The dance idea, though, it's something we've never tried before."

"Oh, I'm sure it will work out. I'll spread the word over at the hotel. Don't forget a lot of the staff hired at the Nirvana will be moving to the area shortly. Your population is about to increase."

"Thanks. I hadn't thought of that."

Ethan paused and eyed her hesitantly. "There are some other options, Lily. For fund-raising."

Lily started for the door. "Jack wants to lock up, Ethan," she said, nodding toward the janitor pushing a wide broom around the perimeter of the room. "Let's talk outside."

He grabbed his leather jacket from the back of his chair and walked with her to the glass exit doors. As they neared the steaming glass the night's blue-black darkness was hung with silver streamers of teaming rain. Buffered by the fog, the red light of the exit sign shone softly through the haze. They stepped out into the glow and huddled under the awning.

"Isn't it beautiful?" she whispered, glancing beyond the parking lot to the white-capped lake.

"Beautiful," he repeated hoarsely, looking directly at her. He cleared his throat. "But where did this weather come from? The sky was clear on my flight out."

She shifted out of the ethereal glow. "Lake effect, Ethan," she informed him, all marine biologist now. "These little bursts blow up from nowhere sometimes. They generally don't last too long.

"I'm just going to give Dad a call. We're sharing the one car at the moment," she mumbled into her purse as she dug for a cell phone.

"I'll drive you home."

Her head lifted and her hand stilled. "No, really. I'll be fine. Dad will pop back and get me." She flipped the phone open and began tapping in numbers.

He reached out and stilled her tapping fingers. Bending his head he looked directly into her eyes.

"Lily. Don't be silly. There's no need for Jared to come out in this downpour. I've got a driver from the hotel picking me up. I haven't had the time to drive out to the Nirvana with my own car yet; I always fly. It's easier just to use the hotel's courtesy car and driver while I'm here. Anyway, I wanted to run an idea about fund-raising by you, remember?"

Her chilled fingers warmed under his touch. Slowly freeing her hands, she deposited the phone back into her purse. Well, it *would* save Dad from coming out in the rain and it *was* business after all. And she really owed it to the group to hear him out.

"Sure, why not? Thanks," she said, nodding her head in acquiescence. She liked the new lighter weight of her hair as it swung easily around her face and she had to admit that Delaney had been right. About her hair, anyway. The more sophisticated style suited her, made her look the way she was beginning to feel. Stronger, more confident.

"Let's make a run for it," Ethan said, grabbing a *Toronto Sun* newspaper someone had left by the door to shield their heads.

Was it today's paper and had he read the

reporter's take on their evening? she wondered as they scurried across the parking lot.

And his matter-of-fact reaction to her refusal to sell wasn't what she'd expected either. He was as hard to read as her father, she thought with annoyance. But now was her chance, and she intended to find out what he really wanted from her.

She ducked under Ethan's arm and sank into the sumptuous backseat of the idling limousine.

Surely the new and improved Lily Greensly—she tossed her hair from her face—could handle sitting next to the suave Ethan Weatherall for a few minutes without losing control of her tumbling emotions.

Chapter Eight

The car smelled of expensive leather and deep roast coffee. The driver straightened, glanced in the rearview mirror and flashed a cordial smile before settling his steaming cup to the center console.

Ethan placed her stack of notebooks and reports at her feet before closing her door and entered the car from the opposite side. "To the Hideaway first, Rick," he informed his driver before sliding the tinted privacy glass closed.

The car eased down Buttermilk Falls' main street and headed north to Loon Lake. An overburdened signpost, listing heavily toward the rail fence, stood sentry at the intersection. Narrow cedar boards, hewn to an arrow point, directed visitors toward affectionately named family cottages. PINE and PARADISE appeared again and again as the eye polled the choices.

The Hideaway's simple wooden sign, a thick oval salvaged from a downed cedar, claimed the top spot. Green boughs partially obscured their phone number, and Lily made a mental note to trim the branches.

A stunning mural-size depiction of the Nirvana stood high and alone on the opposite side of the road. The vinyl billboard gleamed its message through the pelting rain.

The car swept silently through a tunnel of towering pines, the dark night pulling the trees closer. The squeak of damp leather signaled Ethan's shift in position. His arm pressed against hers and her heartbeat quickened. He didn't speak, but she heard a heavy sigh.

"Tired, Ethan?" He had to be. She couldn't imagine flying all the way in from Toronto for an evening meeting.

"I am." He spoke as though he was evaluating his words. "The quietness out here makes me realize just how crazy my life has become."

"But you love your job, right? I saw the look in

your eyes when you gave me the tour of the Nirvana." She searched for his face in the darkness. "It's what you do, what you are."

"I've never been as excited about building a hotel before, Lily." His words came quickly. "It's been my baby from the get-go. I had to convince a lot of people on the board that I could make this hotel succeed."

His tone turned steely as he continued, "Especially my father. He expects nothing less than perfection." His shoulder pressed into hers and she could feel his muscles tighten.

Lily remembered how the offer-to-purchase documents had stated the helipad would become an integral part of the Nirvana's vacation experience. Suddenly his ridiculously high offer for Osprey Island made sense. It was about much more than landing helicopters. It was about perfection.

She placed a tentative hand on his knee and patted gently, deciding she could almost forgive his untimely bid to buy her island.

"Your father's certainly not perfect. He's human too, and after all, you're his son." Jared Greensly had certainly watched her make loads of youthful mistakes over the years. Like getting engaged to Doug Randall, for instance.

Ethan straightened his shoulders and Lily could

feel his bulk fill out his corner of the backseat. "Not every family is like yours, Lily. And I suppose if it wasn't for my father's demanding ways, I wouldn't be here today." A brush of cool air against her cheek told her his free arm swept the interior of the town car, indicating his wealth and position.

"That may be, but there are other kinds of security that matter too. Family is my security. No matter what happens, the support is there. Even when we're not together," she stated simply. She recalled spending a late August afternoon on Osprey Island with Grandpa. They'd been dispatched to pick blueberries but had abandoned their search and stretched out on the flat rocks, naming clouds. Pinpricks of tears started in the corners of her eyes.

You couldn't put a price on memories.

Her eyes searched the dimness for his face. The lines etched on his forehead brought her hand up toward his face but she fought the impulse to smooth away his tension and dropped her hand to her lap. "Ethan," she said softly in the darkness, "you said you had a fund-raising idea?"

"Right. No promises, but I have an associate who might be interested in hearing about your research. His company, the Southerland Group, accepts synopses from groups like yours. You know, stating your mandate, futures goals." He paused and added almost sheepishly, "And like most successful businesses, he's looking for tax-advantageous places to spend money."

"Ethan, that's wonderful," she said. "Tell me more. What's a mandate of a . . . what? And do you mean my research goals or the Friends of Loon Lake's goals? What size of donation are we talking here? I guess it's too late to phone Dr. Nesbitt tonight."

"Calm down, Lily. I said he 'might' be interested in sending some money your way. It'd be up to you to convince him. But I haven't a doubt in the world about your ability to win him over to the green side," he said, his tone admiring.

Lily slumped back, old insecurities settling over her like a wet blanket. "I'm glad you think so, but I've never done anything like this before. The biggest fund-raiser we ever had was an all-day car wash followed by a chicken barbecue at the mayor's house. What if I blow it? Remember, I majored in fish, not finance."

A low chuckle generated from Ethan's side of the car. The gentle shaking of his body told her that he was enjoying her agitation.

"It's not funny," she insisted. "First you throw me a lifeline, then laugh when it misses me by a mile."

"I'm sorry. Don't be mad," he apologized. "It's just that I see you as the perfect person to make the pitch for funds." He sobered suddenly. "You're a bright woman working on the front lines. But your most powerful asset"—he covered her hands with his—"is your passion."

Lily looked up. His face was mere inches from hers. "My passion?" Her voice trembled. Surely he meant for fish. She'd been playing it cool all evening, ignoring him just the right amount. Masking her excitement when he arrived at the meeting. Polite, yet removed.

"You are a rare breed, Lily Greensly," he whispered, lifting her chin with his fingertip. Her pulse quickened and she lowered her eyes, afraid to meet his gaze. "Most people have long since lost any enthusiasm for what they do. I see you as the only one . . . ," he paused, his gaze tangling with her own, and stumbled with his words, "to make the pitch for funds."

Feminine instinct, as old and as strong as the mountains, told her that by midsentence his head had won a battle with his heart.

His breath mingled with hers and her resolve to remain unaffected dissolved. She ached to be in his arms. A tiny sigh escaped from her lips. All ability to continue with pretense flooded from her body and she leaned incrementally closer.

His lips brushed hers—a whisper of a kiss, a butterfly tasting nectar, then flitting away.

Her arms crept to circle his neck and he tugged her closer, as if any space at all was too much. He groaned softly and her lips softened under his kiss. His heart pounded through his shirt, and their kiss deepened.

Doug's kisses had never made her feel this way. Lost in a completely vulnerable and deliciously exciting place, her worries didn't so much fall away as they imploded on impact.

His hand slid into her hair, caressing the back of her head. Her fingers traced the rough stubble of his jawline before winding into his thick hair. The rain cocooned the car with its steady rhythm, its drumming only white noise.

Yellow light burned through Lily's closed eyelids, dragging her back to reality. Rick's voice crackled through tiny speakers set into the thick privacy glass. "The Hideaway, sir."

Lily stared uncomprehendingly at the tinted glass before locking eyes with Ethan once again. They couldn't possibly have covered the three miles from Buttermilk Falls already. Slowly, her hands slid from his neck and Ethan shifted to the side. Pressing a small button beside the speaker he replied in a strained tone, "Thanks, Rick. Keep the car running, I'm walking Miss Greensly to her door."

"There's no point in both of us getting soaked," Lily protested as Ethan struggled to take off his jacket.

He shot her a look that booked no rebuttal and reached across to pop the door handle open. "Let's make a run for it."

He covered their heads with his leather jacket as they skirted the mud puddles already pooling on the graveled path. Taking the back porch steps two at a time they skidded to a stop under a small canvas awning.

Other than the dim bulb burning above the back door, the house was dark. The Greenslys' door hadn't been locked in her lifetime, but nonetheless she rummaged industriously in her purse for keys.

"Here's Pete Southerland's number, Lily." He handed her a business card. "If you like I can help with the proposal. Not that you couldn't handle it on your own."

The philanthropist looking for a worthy cause— she'd almost forgotten all about him. "Er . . . yes. I'd love some help."

"I'm due back in the Toronto office tomorrow afternoon, but how about a breakfast meeting?"

Breakfast with Ethan? In ten short hours? "Sounds good."

"The coffee shop in Buttermilk Falls okay?"

She pushed the door open with her shoulder. "Perfect. I'll be there."

She stuck her nose through the crack. "What time, Ethan?"

"How about I pick you up? Eight too early?"

"I'll be ready."

He peered through the slim opening. "Well. I guess it's good night."

"Yes. Good night and thank you for the ride." Lily called to his departing back, instantly regretting the ridiculously lame remark.

She leaned against the kitchen door and examined the evening. They had been talking business and the next thing she knew she was in his arms. Again.

And no mention of Osprey Island. Wait till Delaney heard about this. But did that mean it was off the table for good?

Hope streamed into her heart. He kissed her because he wanted to, not to sway her decision to sell.

She glanced at the clock. Ten-thirty. She chewed her lip. Tomorrow was Delaney's day to pack her scissors and curlers and visit the seniors in Tay Valley's nursing home. The owner of Buttermilk Falls' beauty shop/art gallery traveled the thirty twisting miles twice a month and put in a marathon day of sets and perms.

Not a good time for a late-night conference with her best friend, Lily decided, and began to spread her damp notes to dry on the table, her gaze lingering on the scrawled details of the dance.

Her hands stilled as she pictured slow-dancing with Ethan on the town hall's deck, a warm breeze drifting in from the lake. In her mind, they swayed to a bluesy love song.

Don't be silly. Her hair flew around her face as she shook her head. He's probably way too busy. She'd glanced his way during the discussion about the dance and he'd looked disinterested, preoccupied. Whatever he had been thinking about, it sure wasn't the dance.

She stood frozen on the black-and-white vinyl tile, the ticking of Grandpa's clock the only sound, and realized she was falling for a guy she knew basically nothing about.

Except that for the moments she was in his arms she felt safe, special.

"Is that you Lily?" Jared Greensly called out in a sleep-heavy voice.

Her hand jerked from the pile of papers. "Yes, Dad. It's me."

Twenty-four-year-old me, who likes quiet country living, drifting across the lake at dawn and eating beans straight out of a can while sitting on the rocky ledges of Loon Lake.

Her life read like an ad in the paper's personals—well, except for the bean lunches, she decided. Just tack on: "Seeking a man who believes in unconditional love and happily ever after." Yes, and the men will be lined up from here to Buttermilk Falls. She snorted softly and began to tread up the worn wooden steps. Pausing at the landing window, she cleared a peephole in the fogged glass with the tip of her finger. She peered into the darkness.

Was there anybody out there for her?

Lights twinkled on from across the bay. She pressed her nose to the glass. It was the first time she'd noticed the Nirvana's lights. A long sigh escaped, refogging the pane.

Was Ethan the one? Longing welled in her heart and she struggled to control the sudden onslaught of emotions.

Her hands balled to fists at her sides. *No. I won't put myself through misery a second time.*

They lived in different worlds, needed different things. He'd never be happy living quietly on the shores of Loon Lake. She wouldn't survive in a noisy, dirty city schmoozing nightly with the who's-who crowd. And how could she expect him to understand the loyalty she felt to her parents and Grandpa Greensly when he was so disconnected from his own?

She plodded upward. Notwithstanding the fantastic kisses, they were completely incompatible. It was hopeless. Anyway, with Osprey Island off the table and the Nirvana almost finished he'd be out of her life soon enough.

Chapter Nine

Ethan maneuvered through stacks of unpacked boxes and plastic-wrapped lobby furniture as he hurried toward the lobby's front windows. Hot coffee sloshed over his fingers, leaving a trail of amber drops to mark his path. But even the disgusting brew from the canteen truck tasted great this morning.

He raised his arm and waved hello to the construction crew gathering on the deck.

He'd fallen asleep listening to the loons and had woken thinking about Lily. It was clear she wasn't mad at him anymore. Her response to his kisses had proven that, but did she trust him? He was determined to keep their private and business matters separate. He wanted her trust, even if she never agreed to sell the island.

He slowed his steps. Abandon the helipad idea? The concept that had brought his father onboard?

Just yesterday, his father had called from England and had inquired about the acquisition. The senior Weatherall's derisive snort had traveled easily from across the ocean when Ethan told him it wasn't a done deal.

He studied the island directly in front of him. There has got to be a way.

Streaks of orange and yellow colored the lake as fingers of light stretched across the bay. A flock of tiny black birds fluttered through his view and quickly disappeared into the dark forest.

Abandoning his island dilemma for the time being, he wondered, could the hotel prepare a directory of sorts for their guests? Something to identify the local birds and animals for patrons who didn't come to the Nirvana just to fish?

He patted his breast pocket for his e-pad and realized he'd left it in his briefcase.

The sun climbed higher. Would Lily guide Hideaway guests later today? He banked down a jealous stirring as he thought of Lily sharing her day with some lucky fisherman.

He checked his watch and his mood brightened. With a final glance to the eastern view he turned and headed to the rear of the hotel and the waiting limousine.

Marion Greensly's head turned toward the sound of crunching gravel. "He's here," she called out to her daughter. "Even his car sounds expensive. My, you're going to make quite a stir when you two pull up in front of the Bluebird Café."

Lily knew her mother was referring to the group of woman who met each morning at the Bluebird for steaming coffee and hot gossip before striking out on their morning constitutional. The Gad-About Girls, mostly blue-haired and dressed in pastel tracksuits, liked nothing better than a fresh snippet of news to discuss while they walked the village streets.

Lily reached for her sweater, a shiver of excitement shooting down her spine, and grinned. "I know. But it's worth it, Mom. If Ethan can help me put a proposal together that will bring money to our project, then it's worth braving the Gad-About's lair."

Marion opened her arms to her daughter and Lily stepped into the embrace. "It's great to hear you so excited," the older woman whispered and gave her a gentle push toward the door.

"I could never do something like that," Lily stated, shaking her head and pressing her palms against the chrome tabletop.

"Of course you can. Everybody does it. I did it before I left the hotel this morning." Ethan shoved his fork into the heaping mound of home fries. "These potatoes are great. I usually just grab a coffee for breakfast, but I'm starving this morning."

"It's easy for you to be so . . ." She searched for the right word. "Offhand. But I'm not sure it's even allowed out here."

He glanced up from his plate at her indignant comment, grabbed a paper napkin, and pressed it to his mouth as laughter shook his body.

Lily knew all eyes were on their table and lowered her voice. "It was only last May when our phone lines were upgraded to Internet capability. And it still takes hours to download files sent from Dr. Nesbitt's office. A three-way conference call with Mr. Southerland in Alberta? I don't think so, mister."

"You may have a point. The lines at the Hide-away probably don't support call-conferencing, but the Nirvana's certainly do. We paid good money for the feed line in from the main highway. Wouldn't have built the hotel without it."

He broke a strip of bacon with his fork as he considered the problem.

His face cleared and he touched the napkin to his lips. "Just use the phone in my suite at the Nirvana."

Lily slumped in her chair before rebounding with, "Why don't I just send Mr. Southerland an e-mail explaining our mandate?" The idea of Ethan listening in while she blathered on to a complete stranger was unnerving, to say the least.

He reached across the table and captured her fidgeting fingers, the laughter gone from his eyes.

"I'm sorry I laughed, Lily, but if my years in the hotel business have taught me anything, it's this: The personal touch, the inside track, the right introductions are essential tools. Use them." His eyes pleaded with her. "Let me help you make that first step. I'll mention a charity golf tournament we both attend"—he threw his arms up, palms flattened—"and then I'll back right off. Hang up, even. You're on your own after that."

She considered his words in silence, aware he was watching as she struggled with her decision.

Did she want to be in debt to Ethan Weatherall? Even owe him a favor? Their relationship was muddied enough. Neither one had mentioned the kiss.

He broke into her thoughts. "The conference call is important. I want you to hear everything I say to him. If he decides to direct some funds to the Friends of Loon Lake it will be your doing, not mine. All credit goes to you."

Could she turn down this opportunity and live

with the consequences? She glanced through the window toward the Tay River that fed into Loon Lake. The water trickled over the glistening rocks. The bubbling falls the village was named after only appeared in the early spring, during the spring runoff.

"Maybe if I wrote out some notes first, you know. In case my mind goes blank," she said tentatively.

He smiled and tipped his head to the side as he studied her face. "I knew you had it in you. Last night, when you were talking about your work, your face lit up, your hands were flying. All eyes were on you, and I bet you didn't even notice."

A blush of color warmed her face and she shook her head. "That was easy. I knew everyone."

He pushed a large envelope toward her. "I printed off Pete Southerland's bio for you. There's personal and business stuff in there. Put you more on an even footing in the conversation."

"Thanks." She slid the envelope from the table into the cotton bag nestled between her feet. "That actually helps a lot. Is there a picture of him in there?"

"There is. A shot of him with his wife and children, I believe." Ethan smiled, apparently very pleased with his attention to detail.

"Okay. I'll do it." Lily pushed her plate to the side with a shaking hand.

"I'll have Callie, my assistant, call you later today with the details." He slid his hand into his pocket and produced a key. "Go ahead and let yourself into my office. I'll tell the crew you'll be dropping in later today.

Lily felt for the thin strip of web cord around her neck and pulled a bunch of keys from under her sweater. Each small bronze key had a number, one through seven, written in black marker. They clanged against the chrome edge of the table as she pried the metal hoop apart and added the slim silver key.

"The key to your young man's heart," Hilda proclaimed loudly as the Gad-Abouts milled around the cash register. Hilda was considered the comedian of the group.

And I was so close to getting out of here. Lily smiled at the group and quickly countered Hilda's wit. "It's just the key to his office. You see, I need to—"

"No need to explain, dear. Not our business what you young people are up to these days." Hilda shot a glance to her band of followers, most of whose penciled brows had raised a fraction, and like a mother hen attending to her chicks, urged them toward the door. "Have a good day, you two," Hilda cooed as the screen door slapped closed.

Ethan set his fork on his empty plate and patted his midsection. "Excellent food. I'll have to remember this spot." He cast a perfunctory glance around the room.

Lily followed his gaze and wondered what he really thought of their only restaurant.

The room wasn't quite vintage, just a hodge-podge of older pieces punctuated with tacky flea-market finds. A counter, lined with bar stools, faced a wall covered in dusty souvenir calendars and post cards. A bulletin board smothered in business cards swung precariously on a single nail. The room's open area was populated with red-topped chrome tables, each surrounded by a mix of plastic stacking chairs. The cash machine, wedged against the till, hummed and clicked industriously, while a couple of carpet steamers, their daily rental rate added to the bottom of the menu placards, lurked in the hallway leading to the bathrooms.

"Look, I need to take off," Ethan said, pushing away from the table. "My plane is fueled and waiting over at Martin's Airstrip, but I'll look forward to our call later today." His questioning gaze asked for something, but she wasn't sure of the answer.

Seconds ticked past. Somebody had to say it. "When are you coming back, Ethan?" She hated how much his answer mattered to her.

"I'm meeting with the public health inspector out here about the septic system on Friday," he supplied eagerly. Flipping open his PalmPilot, his eyes raced over the dates. He peered at the tiny digital numbers. "At ten thirty. Hopefully, that won't take long."

"Oh, I'm sure everything will be fine. You followed the code to the letter," she tossed out nonchalantly. Only two days to wait, she thought, a smile on her lips.

"Would you like to go on a picnic with me?" she blurted out. "On Friday, after your meeting. You know, in return for breakfast." She nodded toward their vacated table, already reset for the next customer.

His hand returned to his breast pocket again. His fingers touched the edge of the day-timer and held there for a second. "Sounds great, Lily," he answered without removing the device. He stuffed his hands into his pockets, a casual stance she hadn't thought him capable of, and looked past her face to the horizon. "I've never been on a picnic, believe it or not."

"You're kidding." As far as she was concerned, it was the best way to eat a meal.

"Why don't you come by the Nirvana on Friday," Ethan suggested. "Around eleven thirty?"

"Perfect." It's just to thank him for his generosity,

she told herself, justifying her impulsive offer. *I'll take him to Osprey Island.*

It was her turn to share a piece of her world. *Who knows, maybe it'll help him understand why I can't sell the island?*

"Thanks for breakfast. And your advice." Lily knew she should stop talking now, but continued as they exited the café. "And for the ride home last night." *Stop babbling and let the man leave.*

Their shoulders brushed companionably as they rounded the corner. "I was happy to do it," his deep voice murmured into her hair as he draped an arm across her shoulders. An empty street stretched before them. No sign of the Gad-Abouts.

"Seems we're alone for the moment."

Lily's head swiveled, assessing the street for subversive activity. You never knew where Hilda and her band of followers might be lurking.

Ethan cleared his throat and reached for her hand. Her heart skipped a beat and the sun slipped free of the clouds that had held it captive all morning. A perfect morning, all around.

"Lily, would you go with me to the . . . Aquatic Ball?"

His body was so close, if she turned her head even a fraction, they would be nose to nose.

She turned.

"You want to go to our fund-raiser?" Her heart

thudded so loudly in her chest she wondered if he could hear it.

He nodded. "I'd like to, with you. What do you think?" He met her eyes for a second and then looked away. "Or maybe I'm too late. Are you already spoken for?"

"No. I was, well . . . never mind about that . . . , she stuttered. "Yes. I'm free. Free as a bird."

Chapter Ten

"**S**o it's off to the Wedding Cake, is it Lil?" Jared teased his daughter. Word is you've got the keys to the joint."

You had to give Hilda credit. She worked fast. "Just one key, for one day, and you know perfectly well why, Dad."

Jared's voice dropped to a more serious tone, "Your mother and I are so pleased you're working right here on Loon Lake. It's a shame to see our lakes ailing." He looked across Greensly Bay to the far shore. "I'm proud you're doing something about it."

Lily balanced herself in the center of the runabout and began to sort the contents of the crowded

117

boat. She'd just returned from the shoal in front of Turtle Point and Ed had left the boat in shambles, as usual. He tended to get overexcited when he got a bite and had tipped the minnow bucket and tangled the extra rods as he reeled in a nice two-pounder.

She hoisted her tackle box to the weathered planking and plunked it at her father's feet. "It's not just me, Dad. I've got backing from U of T and Dr. Nesbitt. And you know how important the Friends of Loon Lake have been. And not just with money. Did I tell you that the Campbells let me set up the rain gauges on their new wharf?"

Jared accepted a selection of fishing rods from Lily and settled them next to the tackle box. "They're fine people. Loon Lake's got more than their fair share of fine folk." He nodded toward the peaks of the Nirvana. "There's another one right there."

Obviously Ethan had been a huge hit with her father. Whatever he had said at the barbecue had won Jared Greensly over.

"I think you're right, Dad," Lily spoke softly. "The Weatheralls won't do the lake or us any harm." She was surprised to realize she meant every word.

Should she tell her father about the Weatheralls' offer? She hadn't mentioned it yet. He had enough to worry about. And there was no point in getting her parents and most likely the whole town in an uproar.

Who knows, the Hideaway's patriarch might even encourage her to sell, not wanting to hold her back from financial freedom. Either way she would keep the offer to herself for the time being.

She watched her father walk to the end of the dock and ease to a sitting position, his work boots only inches from the lapping waves. He began to weave the frayed ends of tie-rope back into itself.

Lily remembered his meeting with Henry Faulkner and wondered how it had went.

"Dad?"

Jared pushed his cap back and raised an eyebrow.

"How are we doing, you know, financially? Everything all right?" She hoped her question came off as casual, offhand.

Jared returned his attention to the rope, twisting the nylon tightly in his hands. "We've been tight before. We'll pull through, Lil."

Lily gaze fixed on her father's back as she absorbed his answer. His tone had been heavy, tired.

"Dad? Is there anything I can do?" An uneasiness rolled through her. "How about I add on more bird-watching excursions? We can rent the Pattersons' pontoon boat again, and I'll take fifteen, maybe twenty customers," she offered eagerly.

"No need to worry, Lil. Just go make your fancy conference call and catch me a nice pickerel on the way back. Your mother has her heart set on fish for supper tonight." He rose slowly and toed the heap of rods. Separating his daughter's favorite from the bunch, he deposited it back into the bow of the runabout.

Reluctantly accepting this as the end of their conversation, Lily pulled hard on the outboard's cord. How can you help someone you love when they won't share their worries?

The tip of her sneaker-clad foot dug into the Nirvana's gleaming hardwood floor, and the black leather chair began to spin. She closed her eyes to fully experience the ride to Executive Town.

The spinning slowed to a stop but she remained mired in his chair and inhaled the room's ambience. It smelled like him. She sniffed again.

Understated extravagance was everywhere. The sparkling crystal water jug, the sleek credenza and matching chairs, the teak bookcase filled with first editions and leather-bound reports.

Her gaze landed on the phone and she wiggled to the edge of the chair and glanced at the row of clocks hung above the entrance. Two minutes. She watched the second hand circle the face. Twice. Nothing.

She scanned her notes, spread neatly across Ethan's desk, and drummed her fingers against the smooth surface. She eyed his Rolodex, surprised a man so married to techno-gadgets still used one. She ran her finger across the polished wooden case. Was she in there?

The soft burr of the phone and a blinking light on the unit drew her back to Ethan's office.

She filled her lungs and exhaled slowly and reached for the receiver. "Hello, Lily Greensly speaking," she said in her most professional manner.

"Lily, it's Ethan. I take it you had no problem accessing my office?" His thoughtful tone calmed her immediately. "Was the foreman there to open the main foyer?"

"Er . . . no. But I managed," she said, stating the obvious. "Mr. Weston, your plumber, let me in through the back entrance. Said he'd keep an eye on the runabout for me too. High winds whipped up after lunch." Was Mr. Southerland listening to their pleasantries?

Apparently he was. "Lily, I'm pleased to meet you," a voice boomed in her ear. "Talk about high winds. Out here on the prairie the wind sounds like a train coming down the track. Never arrives though." He chuckled at his own joke.

Lily sank back and kicked off her sneakers. Resting her feet on Ethan's desk she smiled into the receiver.

She listened attentively as the two men discussed the rebounding market and the upcoming Trillium Open Golf Tournament. Suddenly the conversation swung back to her.

"Lily, I'll see you Friday." Her feet hit the floor. "And . . . be careful going home. Ask one of the crew to give you a lift in the company truck if the lake looks too rough." The concern in Ethan's voice was audible.

There he goes again. Mr. Southerland is going to think he's my boyfriend or something, she thought, panic rising in her throat. Oh wait, Mr. Southerland is in Alberta—not Buttermilk Falls, she remembered. So it doesn't really matter.

"Okay, Ethan. Thanks." A tiny click indicated he'd exited the three-way conversation.

Line One continued to blink. I'm on my own now, she realized and bent to her notes. She plucked a pen from behind her ear and rolled the chair closer to the desk.

With Ethan no longer listening in, her confidence rose and she addressed the man she hoped would soon be Loon Lake's benefactor. "Mr. Southerland, let me tell you something about my work."

"Please do." His tone was serious. "I'll tape this

Lily, if you don't mind. I'll need to run your proposal by my board and I want the stats to be accurate."

"Absolutely. That's a good idea as I'll be sharing a lot of statistics and dates with you."

Thirty minutes later she replaced the receiver into its cradle. Lily checked the clock and was shocked at the time displayed. Had they really been on the phone that long?

She pushed her hair behind her ears and surveyed the mess on Ethan's desk. Reports were strewn everywhere.

Mr. Southerland had queried her every statement. She'd doubled back and searched her notes time and time again to find answers to his surprisingly knowledgeable questions. No wonder he was the most successful entrepreneur in western Canada.

She knew she'd handled the academic portion well, but wondered what he'd thought of the latter part of their conversation.

Whenever anyone asked why she cared so much about the survival of the local lakes, passion overrode objectivity. She spoke from the heart until she reached her listener, at least on some level.

And her answer to what she hoped to gain from an influx of cash? That one had been easy.

Clean water. Protected shorelines. Lakes where not only fish could thrive, but people too. Like she did.

She nibbled on a fingernail. *I hope I didn't bore him. Not everybody cares about the environment like I do.* Delaney fondly referred to her pleas for conservationism as rants.

And she'd come away with another contact. Mr. Southerland had given her the name of a philanthropist based out of Montreal. Apparently his friend, Mr. LaPierre, regularly donated money to environmental causes as well.

Her gaze dropped to the thick writing paper topped with the Nirvana logo. The page was covered with her handwriting. Her fingertip tracked across the millionaire's Montreal phone number. Mr. Southerland was going to speak to his friend later today, and then it was back in her ballcourt.

Lily kicked off the spinning chair again. The things she could accomplish with adequate funding were significant! For the first time she could actually envision her dreams coming true.

Hey, she realized, with a smile, the business side of saving the world was kind of fun.

Her hand reached across the desk toward the phone. She couldn't wait to tell Ethan. If it hadn't been for him, none of this would have happened.

I hope he's still in his office, she thought as she pecked out his number.

Now, the prospect of going to Montreal to further push her cause seemed exciting. What a difference one morning can make in your life, she marveled.

His office phone burred in her ear. "Mr. Weatherall's office," a friendly female voice answered.

"Is Ethan in, please?"

"No, I'm sorry. He's out of the office. May I help you with something? It's Callie, his assistant."

So this was the efficient Callie? She sounded younger than Lily had imagined.

"No, I don't think so." She spoke hesitantly. "Just tell him Lily Greensly called and that everything went well. He'll know what I mean." Her excitement dropped a notch. Ethan obviously had more pressing business matters requiring attention.

"Lily! So nice to speak with you at last."

He's talked to Callie about me? A flush warmed her face.

Callie's tone became confiding. "The boss came back from Loon Lake a new man. Relaxed, whistling even."

"Mmmm, that's great." *Is she implying I had something to do with his improved mood?*

"I'll pass along your message, Lily. He's out on a date with Emma," Callie said, her voice sweet and light. "Said he was taking a long lunch. You know how it is. Trying to make up for all the time away at the Nirvana. That gal of his keeps him in line."

Callie's bantering may have continued but Lily

was no longer listening. A cloud blanketed the sun and she felt cold. She scanned the room for her discarded sweater.

Had Ethan mentioned this Emma? Most definitely not; she would have remembered even a vague allusion to a girlfriend.

The line buzzed softly in her ear. "Lily?"

"I've got to go. Thanks, Callie," she choked out before clattering the receiver to its cradle.

She huddled into the soft leather of Ethan's chair, pulling her knees to her chin. She wrapped her arms around her shins and turned to face Greensly Bay.

The effects of Callie's bombshell washed over her again and again. Waves of anger deluged her body, leaving dregs of disappointment behind each time.

Tears pooled in her eyes. She straightened her legs and flung herself from the chair. It rocked uneasily for a moment before rolling, empty and silently, across the wood floor.

All he did was kiss me, she reasoned, while pacing between the window and the desk. He didn't promise anything. He asked me to be his partner for the dance, not for the rest of his life.

Logic was fast losing ground in its battle with her rising humiliation. The darkened sky rolled ominously and a gust of wind drove a spitting rain against the pane. Tears spilled and rolled down her cheeks.

Doug's defection had taught her a painful lesson. Several actually. She required a man who could commit for now and forever. A man who could put roots down here on Loon Lake. Because she couldn't survive anywhere else.

She remembered how her skin had warmed when Ethan had smoothed a strand of hair from her face, how when he looked into her eyes she'd felt as if he was mining her soul.

There was no denying her feelings: she was falling for the guy. Her hands clenched in to balls of steel. But it wasn't too late to pull back, to hang on to her dignity. She'd go to the dance with him, but keep it cool and light. There was absolutely no way she'd let herself fall hard for a high-roller, girl-in-every-hotel kind of guy.

Chapter Eleven

Lily punched her pillow into a ball and flipped to her back. She rubbed her eyes, gritty from her sleepless night, and gazed around her childhood room.

Topographical maps and charts were tacked haphazardly on the thick log walls. When most girls were into boy bands she'd invested her allowance in the Fishes of Ontario calendar series, a must-have collection produced by the Ministry of Natural Resources.

A state-of-the-art computer and an enormous steel file cabinet claimed one entire wall.

This is my life, she realized. She rolled to her side and squinted at the clock.

Five forty-five.

Time to get up. Ed would be on the dock, fishing rod in hand by six. She stuck her feet into a pair of worn flip-flops and stood. Usually she bounded down the stairs, anxious to beat the sun to her favorite honey-holes. Today it seemed, well, like work.

"Lily," her father called from the kitchen below. "Got a minute this morning? I need to talk to you."

His voice sounded strange. Forced.

The back of her neck tingled as she padded quickly down the back stairs. He never announced when he wanted to talk, they just talked. The only other time he'd asked for her attention was when he told her that her mother's failing eyesight had advanced to the point of blindness.

"What's up?" She snatched a piece of toast from the buttered stack in the middle of the table and leaned against the counter. Her father sat in his spot at the head of the table, his hands cupped around his coffee cup.

He cleared his throat.

Lily stared at her father's bent head, willing him to speak, her toast cooling in her hand.

"Honey, now I don't want you to worry too much about this but I have some bad news. Henry Faulkner called yesterday." Jared cleared his throat again. "Between the taxes and the upkeep on the place and well . . ." He spread his hands and pressed them into the tabletop. "We aren't going to be able to afford to keep the Hideaway up and running. This will be our last year. He advises we take advantage of the rising value of lake property and . . . sell."

"Dad," she breathed. "No. There's got to be another way."

"It's no use, honey. He's been worried about the lodge for a couple of years now, but figured things would turn around. Always did before." His voice was flat. "He knows his stuff, Lil."

They'd been in financial trouble for years? He'd carried his worries alone, she realized, doubting he'd even told her mother.

"Don't worry," he said, a smile stretching tautly over his lips. "Maybe your mother and I will buy a little house in Buttermilk Falls and start enjoying ourselves. You'd still be close enough to the lake to do your research too. But it's time I retired, don't you think?"

She attempted a smile. *No,* a voice in her head shrieked, *you're only fifty-seven, Dad. This lake, this lodge, is your life. Cut your veins and Loon Lake's water pours out.*

Not to mention he'd die of boredom stuck in the village all day.

She padded across the linoleum and placed a hand on his shoulder. He clamped his calloused palm over hers and squeezed. She hoped he didn't notice the slight tremor in her touch.

Suddenly the kitchen felt suffocating. Like her father, when she needed to think things through, she did it outside.

She knew Ed was already on the dock. The clunking and banging coming from the shore meant he was loading the boat without her. Never a good thing.

Jared dropped a sugar cube into his wife's coffee mug, collected his own from the counter, and headed upstairs to his wife. "Get to work now, Lil. Ed will have your boat all messed up before you even cast off, if you don't get out there soon." He leveled a glance in her direction. "None of this is happening today, hon. You never know, maybe money will drop out of the sky. I just thought you deserved a heads-up."

Lily puffed an errant strand of hair as she strode the familiar path to the dock. The path Greensly guides had been stepping on for three generations.

Her eyes inventoried the shabby cottages, the dented boats, and the much-mended nets hanging on the weathered clapboard boathouse with the critical eye of a real estate assessor or a money lender.

Sure, the Hideaway had seen better times, but she wouldn't give up. Not now, not ever. Grandpa Greensly built this place with his own hands, and she'd find the money someway, somehow.

Chapter Twelve

They sat cross-legged, three rows of color blocks between them on the ancient quilt. A chilling mist lathed their faces each time the wind gusted across Greensly Bay. The small granite bulge that was Osprey Island felt huge today as the silent pair drained their raspberry juice boxes.

Ethan glanced toward Lily, surprised by her low spirits. After all, she was Nature's child, more likely to wax romantic than complain about Loon Lake's fluctuating weather. Even he, an unabashed city-slicker, found pleasure in just sitting beside her on the rock, whatever the weather.

"Lily? You seem . . . preoccupied. Are you sure you're up to this?"

Her blond hair tumbled against her cheek, shadowing her face as she nodded her head. "I promised you a picnic and here we are," she said, her smile not reaching her eyes.

Apprehension pumped his pulse and he abruptly switched gears. "I heard from Southerland. Looks like you won him over with your presentation. He was really impressed with your work. Your vision."

She lifted an eyebrow. "He said that?"

Encouraged, he continued, "He recommended you meet with LaPierre too. He wouldn't have done that without good reason. I knew your passion would blow him away."

"Well, I don't know about that," she murmured, sealing the lid of the macaroni salad with the tip of her finger. "Sometimes all the fire in the world isn't enough."

Why did he get the impression they were talking about two different things?

She turned to face the lake. Her golden freckles, quickly becoming his most favorite feature, stood out against her pale skin.

Was she sick? He shrugged out of his jacket. "You look cold. Here, take this," he said and draped it around her shoulders.

Thanking him with a perfunctory nod, she thrust her hands into the jacket's deep pockets.

"Achhh," she screamed, ousting a furry lump from the side-slit pocket and flinging it toward the lake.

"Clarence!" He dove for Emma's stuffed animal as it ricocheted off the granite and bounced to the ledge. Emma without Clarence wasn't something he wanted to contemplate.

Finally, a practical use for the island's prickly juniper bushes, he thought, as a branch snagged Clarence's ear. Ethan plucked the worn teddy bear from the plant and jammed it into his pack.

"Emergency averted," he said, a stain of color warming his face as he dropped to the blanket.

Still shaking, Lily glanced toward the pack and back to his face, confusion and fear clouding her eyes. "Ethan?"

He knew what he needed to say to ease her mind about the stuffed toy, and that he'd already waited far too long. But the story was stored down deep—in a place he didn't want to visit.

His gaze slipped past her huddled form to the end of the bay. Even from here, he could make out the Hideaway's weathered sign rocking in the wind. And he decided if anyone understood family loyalty, it was Lily Greensly.

He cleared his throat and began, "There's someone in my life you need to know about."

Even though Callie's offhand remark had tipped

her off, his words sent goose bumps torpedoing up her arms and she shrank deeper into his jacket, protecting herself from both the cold and his words.

"I have a twin sister. Emma." He nodded toward his backpack. "I must have put Clarence, her stuffed toy, into my pocket this morning when I was saying good-bye."

Struggling to make sense of his words, Lily clung to her anger. *"Sister? Twin?"*

She knew he had to be in his early thirties. She stared into his face and waited for the truth.

"It's a long story, Lily. One I should've told you sooner, but when your every move ends up in the society pages, you become . . . guarded."

Having a sister wasn't news, Lily knew, so why the caution? She nodded for him to go on. "I'm listening."

His knuckles whitened as he tightened his grip on his bent knees. "I work hard to keep my private life private. Emma is off-limits to everyone except my closest friends."

Obviously his assistant, Callie, fell into that category. The needle-end of jealousy pricked her heart.

He paused for a breath. "Emma has Down syndrome and needs lots of care." His eyes searched her face for a reaction. "But mostly she just needs security. Love."

Her fingers unclenched, her head tipped to the side as his words soothed the fear Callie's words had created.

"Emma's your *sister*," Lily repeated. "And she lives with you." She wondered briefly about his parents.

His behavior began to make sense. He confided in Emma, he had *long lunch dates* with Emma.

She leaned in, longing to offer comfort, to touch him. His jacket slipped unnoticed from her shoulders, the off-shore breeze now invigorating, fresh. Her intuition had been right. He was one of the good guys.

She spun to face him. "Tell me more. I've always wished I had a brother or sister. And a twin, no less!"

Ethan looked relieved. "What do you want to know?"

She asked the obvious. "Why is she with you?"

His voice took on an edge. "Have you ever seen a child's face when they've been told their mother has left? Isn't coming back?"

Like a spray of icy water, his words caught her off guard and she shifted against the hard rock.

"Our mother took off when we were six. Father was busy building his hotels. Never had any time for us. He was really angry . . . embarrassed maybe, when she left. Your guess would be as good as mine," he added bitterly.

"We had no one," he continued. "Father wasn't around. Just kept throwing money at the paid help." His voice was stronger now, but still tinged with bitterness.

"Eventually, he separated us. Emma and I. Put her in an institution and enrolled me in a prep school. After school and nearly every day for the next eleven years, I went to Emma's hospital.

"The day we came of age, I accessed my trust fund and brought Emma home. For the last fourteen years we've shared my condominium."

Lily shook her head, his story almost incomprehensible. Her hand reached to his face. Gently, she stroked his cheek, her thumb sliding along the line where the beginnings of his beard met his lightly tanned skin. The hard ridge of tightened muscle softened under her touch. He loosened his hold from his knees and placed his hand over hers, drawing it down and tucking it against his middle.

"Thank you," she whispered. "I know telling me couldn't have been easy."

He turned to face her directly, as if anxious now to explain everything. "I've told Emma about you. About your job, your boat," he slapped his palm against the granite, "Osprey Island, even."

He hitched his jacket up around her thin shoulders again and pulled her closer and went on. "I think looking after Emma actually made our loss a little easier."

"But you were just a child yourself," she spouted in his defense. Her childhood had been filled with days of skipping rocks and nights of dreaming of mermaids and princesses . . .

"It probably was the impetus for the success of my career." He spoke calmly now.

Still, Lily wanted to wrap her arms around him, take away the pain.

"I needed to be sure I'd always have the money to keep Emma with me. Our father picked up the tab for the institution, of course, but when I brought Emma home, against his better judgment, she became my responsibility."

"How could he be so cold-hearted," she blurted out.

"After Mother left, he just couldn't cope."

Pinpricks of tears stung her eyes and she searched for the words to express her tumbling emotions. Only trite platitudes came to mind.

"I'm sorry for you and Emma," she finally whispered.

Ethan pointed upward to a large circling bird. "Now enlighten a city-slicker, Miss Greensly, is that a hawk or a crow?" And she knew this particular conversation was over.

They sat shoulder to shoulder on the high rock and listened to the lapping waves.

No wonder he was desperate to own this island, Lily realized. His ambition came straight from his gut.

She squinted toward the opposite shore. There had to be another location for his helicopter pad.

She was perfect, he decided. Any child of hers would be cherished, protected. No matter what.

Who was he to stick a noisy helicopter pad in Lily's paradise? He looked across the bay's blue-black expanse to the Nirvana, and for a moment almost hated the dazzling structure he'd commissioned.

He filled his lungs with lake air and braced for a reaction. Nothing. He carefully drew in a second breath, drawing the air down deep. Not even a tickle. His shoulders shifted back, Lily was right. Her lake really could work magic.

The fact that Lily was still unattached was amazing, he thought. This Doug character, the rat Lily's father had told him about, was a fool. With or without her sight, Lily would always be light years too good for that idiot.

By the time Doug realized his mistake, Lily

would be long gone, he thought with satisfaction. Happily married to some lucky guy. Her adorable blond-haired kids fishing for perch off this very rock.

He turned and suddenly she was in his arms. He didn't remember how she got there and it didn't matter. She was in his arms.

He tugged her closer to his chest. Intoxicated by her flowery fragrance, he sank his fingers into the corn husk silk of her hair and drew in the sweet smell. Cradling the back of her neck with his hand, he tilted her face up to his. Eyes as blue as the sky shone back. His lips moved to graze her eyelids, to caress the tip of her nose, and finally to settle on her mouth. Raspberry punch sticky lips joined eagerly with his, and soon he knew only the sweet taste of Lily.

He murmured into her neck, "I know it's been hard to trust me. Especially after what happened with your fiancé. But . . ."

Lily stiffened in his embrace. "Doug?" she spoke hesitantly. "You know about Doug?"

Her arms loosened their hold and dropped from his neck. He wanted his words back, but it was way too late.

"Let me guess. Dad told you about Doug."

Her irritated tone spoke volumes.

"The night of the barbecue, when your father and I were by the shore, he told me why your engagement ended and that Doug was a self-centered twit. A warning for me, I presumed."

She clamped her hands over her face. "Oh no." She continued to speak through a crack in her fingers, "You and I had only just met. You must have thought Dad was a crazy man."

He gently pulled her hands from her face. "That's not what I thought."

She looked at him expectantly. "What did you think?"

"I thought"—he placed his arms under her knees and scooped her onto his lap—"that I could respect a man who spoke his mind. That I admired a father who protects his family." He placed a finger under her chin and lifted her face to his. "Even then, after only knowing you for a few days"—he dropped kisses on her closed eyelids—"I'd decided that Doug was the one that must be blind."

Her arms crawled back around his neck and she rested her head against his chest. Lulled by the rhythmic beating of his heart, she quietly assessed this new information.

He knew there was a chance she might lose her sight someday. He'd always known. She traced a finger along his jawline. It was strong, determined.

He'd worked hard for years to support and protect his sister. When it came to love and family he didn't require perfection.

She looked to his eyes for the reassurance she needed to open her heart, to let the mistrust seep away.

She smiled, confidence swelling her heart, when he took her hands and grazed them softly with his lips.

Ethan Weatherall would never hurt her.

Chapter Thirteen

Lily directed the runabout south, toward the far end of the lake.

Ethan had returned to Toronto for his Friday night dinner with Emma, promising with a tender kiss to be back in two days, just in time for their first official date, the Friends of Loon Lake fund-raiser dance.

Her father hadn't mentioned the impending sale of the lodge again, and Lily read his silence as a positive sign. Although she suspected her father had now shared Henry Faulkner's grim forecast with her mother.

Now, each evening after supper, her parents walked the trails that meandered through the spruce forest that backed the Hideaway. Hand in hand they visited their favorite landmarks, usually ending their walks lakeside, ensconced in the Adirondack chairs.

When she was a little girl, Lily often had begged for her mother to retell the story of how the handsome Jared Greensly had proposed marriage while escorting a besotted Marion Burrows through that very forest.

She straightened her shoulders. The Greensly family wasn't going anywhere. If she could generate money for marine research, surely she could figure out how to hang on to the family home.

She steered the boat toward the narrows, just off Turtle Point, and cut the motor. She squinted into the high sky. Perfect weather, she decided, and reached for the bobbing red buoy. With practiced ease she attached a shiny aquatic gauge to the lower portion. With the four gauges in place, the water would be monitored twenty-four/seven for harmful toxins and rising phosphorous levels.

"Thank you, Mr. Southerland," she said as she clamped the final gauge to its buoy. His generous donation had already made a difference. And promoting her project hadn't been nearly as hard as she feared.

In fact, she was actually looking forward to the

meeting with Mr. LaPierre, the restaurateur Mr. Southerland had suggested she approach. This second candidate had suggested they meet in Montreal the day after the fund-raiser dance. She should bring her research notes and Dr. Nesbitt's endorsement of the program, he'd said.

A tingle raced up her spine in anticipation of the outcome.

It would appear the elite of the business weren't all cutthroat capitalists after all. She'd certainly been wrong about Ethan.

But the trip to Montreal would steal valuable time from her research, not to mention her guiding schedule, she'd lamented to her father.

Time well spent, he'd reminded her, if she managed to secure a second philanthropist's attention.

She paused, the outboard's start cord wrapped tightly in her fist. If things went her way, she thought giddily, she could be off to Halifax or Vancouver next.

Who knows, perhaps at some point she could organize a demonstration of equipment, show slides and speak to a group of potential investors right here on Loon Lake. *Mmm, a helipad near the Nirvana might not be such a bad idea after all,* she considered. It certainly would make her fund-raising job easier.

She scanned the landscape to the south and east. The unoccupied private cottage lots were all far too narrow to accommodate a landing pad.

She groaned, prompting a clutch of partridge to flutter from their hiding spot under the shore's thick underbrush.

At least if the pad was on Osprey Island it wouldn't intrude on anyone's space. And to be honest, not even the Osprey returned anymore to nest in the branches of the island's only remaining tree.

What did Ethan's offer say about noise control? Something about the company helicopter being equipped with a high-tech, quieter exhaust system? She'd been so angry that night, she'd not taken the time to absorb the details.

But the ridiculously high offer, she remembered.

More than enough to secure the future of the Hideaway. To send the creditors packing. To fix up the cottages, buy a couple of new boats.

Uneasiness crept into her stomach. Her father's optimistic words about money falling from the sky weren't so far-fetched after all.

She yanked on the motor's pull-cord and swung the boat around, gunning for Osprey Island.

Carefully navigating the rocky perimeter of the island, she circled it again and again. A Tarzan rope, frazzled with age, still dangled from a half-dead spruce branch. Blackened patches of soot dotted the rocks, marking past fires lit by three generations of Greensly guides as they'd prepared shore lunches of pickerel and tea biscuits.

Cold tears traced down her cheeks as she recalled her last picnic, five years ago, with Grandpa Greensly. They'd polished off egg salad sandwiches and chocolate cupcakes and talked for hours about her move to the university's student dormitory. He'd been so happy when she told him she'd decided to be a marine biologist.

She swiped the tears away with the back of her hand. Grandpa would understand. He'd never stand by and let the Hideaway be sold to strangers. Not if there was anything he could do to save it.

Before she could second-guess her decision, she headed the boat for Greensly Bay. Hidden in the bottom drawer of her dresser was Ethan's offer to buy the island. If she signed it and sent it by courier today he might even arrive for the dance with a check in hand.

She could hardly wait to see the joy on her parents' faces when they realized they wouldn't be moving into one of Buttermilk Falls' cookie-cutter homes.

She wouldn't tell them though, until the deal went through. Her stubborn, old-fashioned father would never let her sell the island to save the

Hideaway. He considered finances his responsibility. But it was time he realized that she wasn't a kid anymore and could take on the privilege of preserving the Greensly homestead. And she knew she could count on her mother to back her up.

And as for Ethan, it was better to let the document speak for itself. She would behave as a proper, seasoned executive and separate their business dealings from their personal relationship.

Chapter Fourteen

"Mr. Ethan Weatherall. You've been summoned to England," Callie announced in her best imitation of a royal Brit. She waved a printout of his father's e-mail through the air as she swiveled her chair to face her boss. "I've booked you on a flight leaving at three o'clock."

He groaned and snatched the paper from her manicured fingertips. Back in the office for less than an hour and the pace of his day had accelerated with warp speed.

He'd hoped to get home for a few hours before dinner and spend some time with Emma before heading out to eat. He could hardly wait to see her face when he told her she would be joining him on his next visit to Loon Lake.

He focused on the e-mail message. *Ethan,* he read, *I closed the deal with the Burtons. I need you here ASAP to sign off. I'll have a car waiting for you at Heathrow.*

No pleasant sign-off, Ethan noted wryly. *No use wasting niceties on the family. Gotta save those time suckers for people you need to impress.*

He forked his fingers through his hair. In anticipation of his return trip to Loon Lake, he'd already asked Callie to delegate most of the routine stuff to Trey Sullivan, his right-hand man. Trey was chomping at the bit, anxious to move up in the company, to prove himself to the boss. The critical stuff, he'd deal with himself on the plane. The decks were cleared, so to speak. But now, Emma would have to wait. Again.

His father had been working on the Burton merger for months. The deal was worth millions. And as head of Weatherall's Canadian division, he had no choice but to get over to England and sign the thing.

The all-too-familiar cold weight of guilt filled his gut as he recalled the unadulterated respect shining from Lily's eyes when he'd told her of his childhood promise to Emma.

"Book me a car please, Callie," he said through gritted teeth, "I'll call Emma from the plane."

Ethan's stride devoured the dim hallways of Weatherall's London office. A quick glance to his wristwatch confirmed his punctuality.

Nothing annoyed Roland Weatherall more than a tardy arrival. Even when it was his own son.

At the end of the hall the polished oak door of the conference room stood ajar, and he heard his father's booming voice mixing it up with the restrained rumblings of his British counterparts.

"Good afternoon, Mr. Burton," Ethan said, extending his hand.

"Father," he acknowledged his parent with a discreet nod.

"Ethan, right on time," the elder Weatherall noted pleasantly without actually meeting his son's eyes. "Just add your signature to the bottom of pages two through seven and we're in business."

A trio of his father's blue-suited yes-men stepped back to reveal the much-anticipated contract.

"Of course." He accepted the pen and bent to the task. *Good flight, thanks. Emma? She's doing great.*

On the plane he'd downloaded the document and needed only to skim the heavy manila pages placed sequentially on the table.

"Dinner at the club, gentlemen?" Roland Weatherall inquired, raising his bushy eyebrows as he surveyed the somber group. A round of polite declines, peppered with "old boy" and "jolly good of you to ask" platitudes quickly circled the room.

Ethan swallowed a smile. *Apparently they don't want to eat with him either.*

Mr. Burton hurried toward the open door, already pressing a sleek cell phone to his ear. With a dismissive wave, Roland sent his assistants scurrying to their cubicles.

"I guess it's just you and me then," Ethan said, unable to come up with a reasonable excuse to eat Chinese take-out in his hotel room.

"Excellent, son. Over dinner you can bring me up to speed on the Nirvana project."

A deft handoff to the exclusive club's maître d' parlayed into preferential seating adjacent to a massive stone fireplace. Father and son studied their menus intently, oblivious to the scrutiny of their fellow diners. The confident demeanor of the similar featured men had commandeered attention the moment they'd entered the room.

Ethan waved off the hovering waiter and closed his menu.

He was ready to make his announcement. "Father, clear your schedule for the twenty-seventh.

That's the day I reveal the most exciting thing to happen to the hotel industry in years. Big-city ambience meets rejuvenating rural escapism," he said, borrowing the quote from his media release. "The Nirvana opens to the public."

Heads twisted in their direction.

His father smiled broadly and stretched his hand across the table. "The first of many, son. You've got your old man's drive, all right. Let nothing get in the way of success, and you'll make it to the finish line every time." He signaled for the waiter. "A bottle of champagne please."

"There's more." He knew his father's admiration would fade with his next sentence and for a second he debated the wisdom of continuing on. "I'm relocating the helipad site to the local airport."

On the flight over, he'd opened his laptop and checked his land acquisition notes. He'd brought up his proposed alternative to buying Osprey Island—the golf course concept utilizing the land just behind the hotel. A few bumps to work out, but definitely doable.

"Too late, Ethan. You know that. Plus, I stand firm in my opinion that affluent travelers like to see all the bells and whistles—privileges, if you will—that accumulate with wealth. Like helicopters bringing them to their retreat. Trust me on this, I know what works. I've been at it a lot longer than you," he said dismissively.

Ethan ignored the comments and forged on, "The scrub land just back from the Nirvana is owned by the Greensly family too, but they can't access it by road. A right-of-way to the hotel is possible. Legal's working on replacing the island offer as we speak."

Color rushed from his father's collar to his forehead and he settled his menu on the damask cloth with a foreboding calmness.

"Continue. I'm intrigued."

"Your idea of the helipad out front would have worked fifteen, even ten years ago—maybe. But things have changed. People care about the environment and quality of life now. If our clientele are coming all the way out to Loon Lake for a holiday, then the last thing they expect hear and see when they look out their window is a smelly, noisy helicopter." Ethan leaned across the dinner table and looked directly into his father's steely gaze. He spoke slowly and deliberately. "I *am* the demographic, so trust me on this. We want to escape our crazy lifestyles with a slower, quieter pace for a few days or weeks. Golf is clean, green, and relaxing. That's it. I'm not backing down."

His father's left eyebrow lifted.

The two men held eye contact as the waiter

popped the cork and filled their glasses with foaming champagne.

When the senior Weatherall lifted his gaze, pride rather than defiance shone in his eyes. "Two questions, son."

"Shoot."

"Does the change of location affect the bottom line?"

"I estimate we will come in approximately nine percent under original budget." Roland Weatherall raised two fingers to his forehead in a subtle salute.

"And just exactly what happened to you out there in no-man's-land? All this stuff about escaping the rat race."

Was it that obvious? "I've met someone."

Ethan scrutinized his father's face. Decades of fourteen-hour days had etched a network of lines and creases into his skin. Empire-building was a tough business. Anyone who knew R.W. understood work came first.

No wonder mother left; no woman could compete with a mistress like that. An iota of sympathy for his mother nudged into years of banked resentment.

"You're not talking about that fired-up environmentalist the Toronto paper caught you schmoozing with?"

"Yes, I am," Ethan snapped, annoyed the newspaper's take on his relationship with Lily had stayed in his father's mind. "I'm surprised you of all people would fall for that media garbage. Lily Greensly is passionate, smart, determined . . ."

"And let me guess, a gorgeous young woman." A barely concealed smirk crossed his father's face.

Ethan's hands tightened into fists under the overhanging tablecloth, and he fought the urge to dump the fully loaded table into his father's lap.

"Yes, she's beautiful," he said, measuring his words and lowering his tone in deference to the posh restaurant. "But you're dead wrong. I've dated beautiful women before, you know that, everyone knows that. Lily Greensly is different. "She's . . ." The words that would do Lily justice eluded him and he settled on, "Real."

"You're serious about this one?

"I love Lily." With the words out of his mouth, he suddenly felt invincible.

A flash of raw emotion lit his father's dark eyes, and then was gone just as quickly.

"Does she feel the same?"

"I sure hope so." He recalled their picnic on the island and the way Lily had returned his kisses.

Roland Weatherall's eyebrows shot up as he reached for his champagne. "I see." He carefully replaced the drained flute on the table. "And what happens to Emma if this little scenario plays out to the happy ending you no doubt envision?"

Ethan swallowed hard. *I don't need this.* He stood and shoved back his chair. He wouldn't sink so low as to answer the offensive question or comment on his father's sudden concern for Emma. "I've lost my appetite. I'm leaving. It's been a long day."

He tossed his napkin to the table and spun to leave.

"Wait."

His feet mired in the plush carpet. He wanted to keep going but something odd in the older man's tone stopped him.

His back was to his father when he heard the words. "I loved Abby . . . the way you love Lily."

What? Had he heard right? Thirty-two years and it was the first time his father had said his mother's given name.

"Please. Sit down." The color had seeped from his father's face, leaving it drawn, older. "I know you wouldn't desert Emma. It was just a stupid gamble to get you to rethink your relationship with this girl."

Why does he care who I date, Ethan wondered. "I don't need to rethink anything."

"I thought Abby and I would be together forever. But life comes along and changes things."

"Doesn't mean that will happen to me."

"Just hear me out son," the older man demanded

quietly. "We had nothing in common, nothing to keep us together when things got rough."

Nothing but two kids. Bile climbed into his throat. He turned to go.

"She was miserable in my world, and I was too stubborn to change. She gave up her art for me. It turned out to be too big of a sacrifice."

Why is he telling me this? "Lily and I could make it work. Commute. Make use of the darned helicopter over at the airstrip. She wouldn't need to give up anything."

The image of Callie waving his summons to England the second he'd stepped foot in his office this morning cut into his thoughts. And Emma's crestfallen expression when he'd canceled their dinner date again.

There was no such thing as a routine day in his world. The staff might be able to handle the in-house stuff. But running a business was like steering a ship; they ran aground when nobody was at the helm.

His father was still talking, as if now that he'd opened his Pandora's box, he was determined to empty it.

"Abby said she couldn't paint anymore. Had nothing left to give to me or you kids. All artsy-fartsy talk. I paid no attention. I figured she'd find something else to occupy her time eventually." He paused. "And then she was gone."

A cold lump rose in Ethan's throat as he faced his demons. What if Lily grew to resent him and the endless, frivolous society events that were an integral part of his lifestyle? Events that would pull her away from her work and the lake? Would Lily become disillusioned, ache for the peace of Greensly Bay?

What if love wasn't enough to make a relationship work? It wasn't enough for his mother or father and they had been married with two children.

He dropped back into his seat and reluctantly forced his gaze to meet his father's.

The corporate magnate sat slumped in his chair, twisting the thin stem of his champagne glass between his fingers. His expression held regret, sadness.

"I'm sorry I messed things up for you and Emma, son," he said hoarsely, "but men like us can't change—not for anybody."

Ethan looked away and stared unseeingly into the crowded restaurant. This time, for once, he believed his father meant every word.

A maple log crackled in the fireplace as the flames licked hungrily at its edges. R.W. spread his hands on the table and pushed himself upright.

He extracted a sleek wallet from his breast pocket and dropped a hundred-dollar bill on the table before raising his head to speak.

The pain revealed in his father's eyes was undeniable, too tough to look at bald-faced. Ethan turned his head again and the beginnings of forgiveness crept in.

"Marrying Abby," his father said, each word laden with self-loathing, "was a selfish mistake. I hurt the best thing that ever happened to me."

Chapter Fifteen

"That's it. A bit more on the right one, I think," Delaney said, peering over Lily's shoulder and into the bedroom mirror. She nodded her head proudly. "You look like a movie star. Who knew!"

Lily giggled good-naturedly at the jab and leaned in to smooth on another layer of green eyeshadow, taking care to blend it with the darker shade of eyeliner.

For years Delaney had begged her to wear makeup. Said if she had Lily's gorgeous eyes she'd make the most of them.

"Perfect," her friend declared. "Now just wait until you see the total effect. Add the dress and The

Friends of Loon Lake won't even recognize their fearless leader."

Delaney reached into her friend's closet and produced the swishy aquamarine halter dress they had simultaneously shrieked and grabbed for when they'd spied it wedged into the sale rack in Tay Valley's trendiest clothing store. Delaney stroked the folds of the delicate fabric. "The pièce de résistance."

Just for tonight Lily intended to be happy, pushing her regrets about selling Osprey Island to the back of her mind.

Anyway, happiness doesn't come from lakes or trees—it comes from the heart, she reminded herself. A tingle raced up her spine. She glanced at her bedside clock and sighed. Two whole hours until Ethan-time.

"So, when is Ethan supposed to pick you up?"

"Well, he knows the dance starts at eight, so I presume around seven thirty."

"You presume?" Delaney's eyebrows shot up.

"Before he left he told me his schedule was crazy. He's a real hands-on kind of CEO, you know. A detail man, I guess you'd call it. He'd have called if anything had changed." She quickly squashed a wave of insecurity before it could erode her new-found happiness. "He'll make it back in time," she added as she tightened the mascara cap.

Delaney draped the dress across the bed's hand-blocked quilt and hugged her friend. "I'm so happy for you," she whispered into Lily's hair.

"I know you are."

Delaney stepped back and smiled at her protégée. "I'm taking off. Gotta get ready for the dance too. See you there," she trilled as she headed for the back stairs.

Lily plopped onto her bed and stared up at the oak beams.

Selling my island was the right thing to do. It'd been hard, the last couple of days, keeping the secret from her father. But she knew he would have tried to talk her out of selling to the Weatherall chain. Pretend again that he was okay with moving to Buttermilk Falls.

The sudden burr of the phone jolted her back to reality. Seconds later her mother's voice reached the second floor, "Lily, telephone."

Ethan! Still prone, she reached for her bedside extension. "I've got it," she informed her mother and listened for the click. "Hello?"

"Lily, hi." A female voice she recognized, but couldn't immediately place, spoke pleasantly in her ear. "It's Callie. Look, Ethan just called from England."

"England?" *He can't be in England. The dance starts at eight.*

"He sends his regrets but there's no way he'll make it home in time for the dance. He's swamped with work."

Callie chattered on about all the extra work and inconvenience of faxing over his correspondence and rescheduling appointments.

"Callie?"

"Yes, Lily?"

She strove for nonchalance. "When is he coming back?"

The line hummed for a second and she heard Callie shuffling through papers. "He didn't say. I can ask and get back to you."

"No, no, that's all right. I'm sure I'll hear from him soon." The lump in her stomach grew heavier as she fumbled to return the receiver to its cradle.

For a millisecond she hated Ethan's assistant. Callie's lighthearted delivery of the news was like a slap in the face. In a few pithy sentences Callie had destroyed what had been, up until now, one of the most exciting days of her life.

Lily rolled into the bank of pillows flanking the far side of the bed and ran the message over again in her head.

Had Ethan ever mentioned a trip to England? She reviewed their recent conversations. He did say something once about his father living in London. It's probably got something to do with his father, she decided and flopped to her back.

Should I call him? A tiny voice in her head warned her off: he hadn't called her, after all.

Hadn't Callie said something about faxing over his reports and correspondence?

Her pulse quickened. Then he'd probably read his mail . . . from her too? Opened the thick package from the Hideaway, marked *Private.*

Her hands moved to cover her ears as if muffling the throbbing beat of her heart would make the ugly facts go away.

No. I'm being ridiculous, she told herself sternly, drawing air deeply into her lungs.

She fought for composure and pulled herself upright to confront her rising fear. Slowly and deliberately, she began to tick off a litany of days leading to this moment.

Ethan had booked her, under somewhat false pretenses, to take him fishing. He'd wowed her with a fancy suite in his Toronto hotel and had offered to buy Osprey Island. She'd refused. Then he'd shown up unexpectedly at a Friends of Loon Lake meeting and provided fund-raising advice. Next, he wooed her with a moonlight ride in his limo, followed by a cozy breakfast. He'd won her heart over with confidences about Emma.

Her hands balled into fists and pressed into her newly made up eyelids and against the threatening tears.

He'd kissed her like she'd never been kissed before. Made her fall in love.

Mascara-blackened tears spilled over and soaked the pillowcase clutched in her fingers as a final domino, the last in a line of indisputable facts, tipped over: She had signed the offer and he'd bolted across the ocean and from her life, the deed to Osprey Island firmly grasped in his hand.

Chapter Sixteen

"Ethan, what's wrong? Your face is sad."

He dragged his thoughts from the files piled on the coffee table and redirected them toward his sister sitting cross-legged in front of the television.

"I'm fine, Emma. Jet-lagged, I guess." The thirty-six-hour roundtrip to England had done nothing to improve his black mood. "Not ready to dive into this stuff." He poked the stack with his foot and slumped into the soft leather couch.

If he was honest, his thoughts weren't really on work. He'd tried. But when he'd read the file on tanning rooms all he could think about was Lily's face, freckled from the sun. And when he looked over a voice-mail proposal he remembered how

Lily usually sounded out of breath when she picked up the Hideaway's phone, as if she had just dashed in from the docks.

What was she thinking now? he wondered. He pictured Lily, her expression changing from anticipation to disappointment as Callie's words would have hit home. She would have realized then it was over between them.

He shook his head. *I had no choice. Lily deserves so much more.*

In the long run a clean break was best, he assured himself. Painful, but she would move on more quickly that way. Meet some other guy.

His jaw clenched, he grabbed a pillow and heaved it across the room.

"So don't look at that stuff if it makes you so mad," Emma said, pointing to the files.

He stared at Emma uncomprehendingly for a moment, then, "It's what I do. Somebody has to look after the hotels, right?" They'd had some version of this conversation many times over.

"I guess."

"How about this? I'll work for a little while and then we'll go out for lunch together." He wasn't hungry but Emma loved eating out, and he needed something to take his mind off Lily.

Emma leaped from the couch. "Ethan, I love you," she said, wrapping her arms around her brother's neck. I'll go change." She turned before heading down the hallway to her bedroom and stared pointedly at the coffee table and his stack of work. "Hurry up!"

It took so little to make her happy. Just a few minutes of his time. If anyone should understand that time was more important than money, it was him, and yet he didn't share his nearly enough.

Halfheartedly he fingered the paperwork he'd lugged home from London. Better not let Callie find out he hadn't even opened the files and packages she'd conscientiously air-couriered over.

From the top of the listing tower, a thick envelope slid to the floor.

This one's as good as any, he decided and mined the mess on the table for the silver letter opener and slid the blade expertly through the sealed end.

He pulled out the contents just far enough to read the heading. Purchase Offer: Osprey Island, Loon Lake.

Callie must have inadvertently sent it with the rest of the stuff, he thought. About to toss it to the to-be-recycled heap, a flowing blue signature at the bottom of page one drew his attention. *What?* He quickly thumbed through the sheaf. Lily's signature appeared on the bottom of every sheet.

Swiping the table clear with his arm, he spread

the Offer to Purchase across the glass surface and scanned the sheets as if a clue was hidden somewhere in the printed words.

When did she sign it? His gaze dropped to the date at the bottom of the sheet.

He checked his watch and frowned. She'd be out fishing on the lake with some lucky tourist.

Less than an hour ago, he'd instructed Legal to send out his new offer. A withdrawal of the first one was to be drawn up as well and sent directly to Lily. Both packages would arrive at Loon Lake tomorrow.

He strode to the window and stared unseeingly into the cityscape. She loved that island.

The Hideaway's finances were obviously strained, but something devastating had to have happened. Something that required lots of money, and fast. His pulse quickened.

Was she all right? Was it her eyes? Her blue eyes that saw beauty where most saw just ordinary. He swallowed hard, regret and fear burned his throat.

His hands locked into fists as his decision formed. A decision his father couldn't make thirty years ago. *I'm going to Lily. Now.*

"Emma!"

She appeared at his side, stuffing one arm into a

sweater and a purse clutched in the other. "You're done work already? Can we go to lunch now?"

"Change of plans, Em," he said, his statement increasing his determination.

"Where are we going?"

"Where I should have gone days ago."

Emma rolled her eyes at her brother's confusing answer. "Do we at least get to eat when we get there?"

"Run and tell Miss Scott to make up some sandwiches," he said, nudging her toward the hallway. "We'll eat on the plane."

His pilot's voice crackled through the cabin, "Flight plans in place, Mr. Weatherall. We'll arrive in Buttermilk Falls at six thirty-five P.M."

Ethan grabbed the small two-way radio hanging from the ceiling, "Excellent, Bill. Let's do it."

"Roger, boss."

His cell phone burred in his pocket. "Hold on while I take this, Bill," he instructed, and he grabbed for his phone. The number on the screen wasn't Lily's and he debated even answering.

"Ethan, sorry to butt in on your personal time, but I just got a call from Apex Developments in British Columbia. They've upped their estimate for construction of our second Nirvana by thirty percent."

Ethan leaned forward and pressed the phone closer to his ear. "No way, Sullivan. They're out of line," he stormed to his right-hand man. "This is the second time they've tried to—"

"Don't I know it."

"—pull a fast one right before signing." Ethan glanced at his Rolex and factored in the three-hour time difference. "And the last time, Trey." Already he was planning his counterattack. Too bad the file was spread across his condo's living room floor.

"Ethan," Emma interjected, disappointment evident in her tone, "I can tell that's Trey, and he's going to ruin our trip to visit Lily, isn't he?"

Her arms crossed her chest tightly as if to protect herself from his words as she stared him down.

Truth barged into the cabin like a bear through a dollhouse. The dial tone buzzed in his ear as he looked at Emma. Tears threatened to fall, but she valiantly continued to fight them off. After all, she was becoming an expert at coping with disappointment too.

"Trey, pack your stuff and get out to B.C. You know Apex as well as I do. Straighten them out, and there's a bonus in it for you."

Emma dropped her defiant stance instantly and hugged his arm.

Static crackled through the cabin, "Well, boss, what's it gonna be—Buttermilk Falls or the West Coast?"

"Buttermilk Falls, Bill," he said, hoping it wasn't already too late. "I've got a way bigger problem out there that needs fixing."

Chapter Seventeen

"Presenting . . . to Lily Greensly, an Academy Award for her amazing performance at the Friends of Loon Lake dance." With a flourish, Delaney presented to her friend an economy-sized bottle of hairspray. "You had them fooled, sister."

"I was good, wasn't I," Lily agreed, rising from the shop's barber's chair and accepting the bottle of Final Net with a gracious nod.

Since there had been no real way of getting out of going to the dance, at least not without providing fodder for Buttermilk's thriving gossip mill, she'd arrived with her parents, spouting Ethan's excuses to all that inquired.

Amazingly, not only did the Friends of Loon

Lake fall for her carefree performance, some actually expressed sympathy for Ethan. "Poor man," Hilda had said. "We really must send him some pictures of the hall. It looks so beautiful with its aquatic theme." She scurried off on a hunt for a digital camera.

Delaney's voice cut through Lily's melancholy. "Come hang out with me while I catalogue the pen-and-inks I picked up at the show last week."

Delaney parted the panel of beaded curtains and settled at her desk located in the rear of the store. "It's mind-numbingly boring. Not the prints, mind you—the cataloguing."

"It beats going home and looking across the bay at Osprey Island. I imagine any day now barges will start lugging over the materials and equipment for the helipad base."

"You've got his check then, have you?"

"Actually, no. But I'm sure it's on its way." Businessmen like Ethan Weatherall no doubt erase their guilt with their big payouts. "He's rich, Delaney," she said flatly. "Money is the easy part for people like him."

"Have you told your father yet?"

Lily slumped in her seat. "I'm telling him today. Can't put it off much longer. I meant to tell him last night, but I was afraid I'd cry or something."

Delaney pushed a package of chocolate chip cookies across the table toward her friend.

"You know, selling the island is the right thing to do," Lily said, the timbre of her voice strengthening as she explained her actions.

"Really the only choice, for a dyed-in-the-wool Greensly like you," Delaney agreed, her reply based on her own family's long acquaintance with the Greenslys.

"And it forced Ethan to slither out from under his rock before he made even a bigger fool out of me." Lily couldn't help but wonder how long he'd have performed his charade.

I'm not the only one deserving of an Oscar, she thought, unable to stop the memory of their picnic on Osprey Island from returning. Was it really only a few days ago she'd snuggled against him for warmth, secure she'd finally met the real Ethan Weatherall?

"Speaking of snakes and such—how's your hunt for research dollars going?"

Lily straightened. "You know, it's unbelievable. My meeting with Mr. LaPierre yesterday was actually kind of fun. I came home with a sizable donation."

"It's not unbelievable. At least not to me. You kind of light up whenever you start yakking about phosphorus levels and acid rain. People trust your message."

Lily smiled weakly in appreciation. Ethan had pretty much said the same thing. "What can I say, I love my work."

Delaney stared at her friend for a second before blurting out, "So long as you don't use your work, and the lake, to hide out from the world. Again."

Lily knew she was referring to the post-Doug weeks when she'd retreated to her island.

"You know, I'm not going to run and hide this time," Lily said thoughtfully. "I don't have the time. I've decided to join a group of biologists who meet in Toronto each month—"

Delaney's pen stopped moving across the ledger. "I'm impressed."

"And participate in a kind of think tank for marine specialists. Mr. LaPierre told me about the group. And provided me with the name of a third potential investor."

"Sounds like your networking is paying off, in more ways than one."

Lily inched forward in her chair. "Ethan broke my heart, Delaney, but he gave me something too. He helped me see that I'm more than just a scientist."

Her friend nodded agreement and sat back to listen.

"And that's good because in today's reality a scientist is only as good as his funding allows."

"True."

"And if I really want to do my job right, I need to spend as much time chasing down grants and donations as I do on the lake."

"Seems to me you wear both hats equally well."

"I've Ethan to thank for that. He opened the door to a whole other world for me."

Delaney shot her best friend a look a pure amazement. "So you've forgiven the jerk?"

"Are you kidding? I hope I never see Ethan Weatherall again."

Chapter Eighteen

Dusk crept across the water toward the island. Lily sat at the base of the aging tree and watched the cottage lights, one by one, twinkle on along the shoreline. Grandpa Greensly's canoe nudged gently against the rocks, punctuating the tranquility with its rhythmic thumping.

Lily's gaze traveled across the bay and up into the forest. She wondered if over time she'd forget the beauty of this place. Forgive Ethan.

In the fading light, she studied the island's rocky surface. It offered little in substance really, home to only a half-dead spruce and a bunch of prickly juniper. When Ethan paved over it, there'd be no real loss of habitat. Not even a squirrel would miss it.

Her heart tightened in her chest. *I'll miss it.*

She shifted from the base of the tree and stretched out on the smooth rock surface. The day's heat, cached in the granite, radiated through the cotton of her T-shirt. A pair of loons called to each other from opposite shores, their haunting cries carrying the length of the lake. Mated for life, Lily acknowledged dreamily. *We all should be so lucky.*

The minutes drifted by, and Lily's eyelids grew heavy. Sleep had been hard to come by since the night of the dance. She gave over to her sleep-deprived body's demand for rest and drifted off.

"Lily."

She stirred. A deep voice from up above dragged her out of her sleepy fog. She twisted against the unforgiving rock and turned her head. A large pair of spotless deck shoes grazed her nose.

"Ethan?"

Her mind dull with sleep, she remained motionless and allowed her gaze to travel the length of his denim-clad legs up to his wide shoulders. He seemed taller than she remembered, his face a pale, blurred mask—and then she remembered everything.

Anger and hurt bubbled in her chest as she studied his looming silhouette. Yeah, he was a lighthouse of a man, luring the lovelorn into unsafe harbors.

"Lily, are you all right?"

She scrambled upright and scanned her surroundings. Junipers, Grandpa's canoe, Ethan . . . all shifted before her eyes.

"I'm fine," she said, leaning back against the tree. "And by the way, this place is still officially mine. I can sleep here all night if I want." *What's he doing here anyway?* She'd nothing left for him to take.

"It's yours forever, Lily. I didn't sign the deal. I didn't even see your signature on the papers until this morning."

His voice was clear, but his words were completely confusing to her. "What?"

"I mean, I officially withdrew my offer for the island this morning," he said more slowly. "But I decided days ago that I wouldn't put a helipad here."

Her heart began to race. "You won't? Why didn't you phone me from England then? Why did you disappear?" Her questions darted across the space between them, targeting the truth. She'd settle for nothing less this time, no matter how much it hurt.

He stepped closer and reached for her hands, holding them tightly, as if he thought she might bolt from his grasp.

"I love you," he blurted out.

He loves me. The three simple words she'd been

aching to hear sank into the void between their bodies, a space crowded with betrayal and fear. She struggled to find a reason to trust his words.

"That's why you left? I don't understand." He hadn't been acting like a man in love.

"Someone temporarily convinced me that Weatherall men don't deserve women like you. I thought I'd just end up hurting you and that a clean break was kindest," he said, shaking his head from side to side. He tipped her chin up with his finger and leveled his gaze directly into her eyes. "I made a huge mistake."

He was here. He loved her. A flicker of excitement lit her heart. She waited, knowing he had more to say.

"I'm *not* my father," he continued, his gaze not leaving her face. "I want my legacy someday to be . . . a happy family, not just a chain of hotels." He waved toward the Nirvana, its towering walls shimmering in the moonlight.

"I fought long and hard to make my mark, and I'm not done yet, but it doesn't all need to happen today," he said, capturing a strand of her hair with his fingers and tucking it behind her ear.

He loved her. He stood her up—because he loved her. Relief watered her knees and she folded into his chest. His arms tightened around her as "I love you too" fell from her lips.

"Got time in your schedule to spend with a vacationing CEO?"

Was he kidding? He'd never spent more than a day or two at Loon Lake before. Lily pulled back to check his face. "You mean you don't have to rush back to Toronto? Or London? Or . . . anywhere?"

"No. Not for a couple of weeks anyway. I told Trey to take over for a while. Gave him complete responsibility until I get back."

"That's wonderful," she said, nestling into his arms. "I'll put you to work out here. What do you know about counting walleye fingerlings?"

His laughter drifted over her shoulder and dropped to the placid water surrounding the island. Her heart swelled with secret pleasure, knowing the lake would carry his laugh to the far shore, bringing heads up and smiles to all who heard.

"I'm thrilled there won't be a helipad here," she whispered into his neck, "but I need to sell this island—to somebody. It's either the island or the Hideaway. Dad's in real financial trouble."

"Hang on. I stopped to see your parents before coming here and told them about my original offer for the island, and then I presented your Dad with a different offer. Oh, and by the way, I left Emma with them and borrowed a canoe."

Ethan in a canoe? *He really must love me,* she thought, giddy with relief.

And Emma with Jared and Marion. A perfect combination. Dad probably had the checkerboard out, while her mother bustled from the kitchen to the screened porch with bowls of her famous apple-crumble in hand.

"I asked your father if he'd consider selling me the acreage east of the Nirvana."

"Dad's back-forty of scrub land? You can't even drive to it. It's useless."

"I'd hoped he'd feel that way too, and I was right. He jumped at the chance to unload it."

Surely Ethan wasn't making a grandiose gesture just to please her?

"My acquisitions department assures me a right-of-way is possible—leading right to my back door. In fact, the property is big enough for a par-four golf course. It's worth a small fortune to Weatherall Enterprises."

He cradled her against his chest as the tears flooded from her eyes. "Hey," he whispered into her hair, "that's good news, sweetie."

Her head bobbed in agreement.

"Now, I see there's another empty lot"—he pointed to a clearing on Turtle Point—"that looks interesting."

"I know the one you mean. Fabulous view. Probably the best view on the lake. It's zoned as residential, though. Weatherall Enterprises couldn't build anything there."

"I know. Perfect spot for a home though, don't you think?"

"Absolutely," she replied, searching his face for the point of this strange yet intriguing conversation.

"Trey's going to take on a bigger role in the company from now on. I don't need to be in the Toronto office more than a couple of days a week. Half of what I do could be done from a home office."

She felt him draw in a breath and he continued talking. "I love it out here. I'm going to build a permanent home here on the lake. I told Emma on the flight out."

"That fabulous, Ethan," she said enthusiastically, not a bit surprised he'd included his sister in his plans. "Emma will love it out here. But just so you know, Ethan, *I'll* be traveling a bit more now," she said, snuggling against his chest. "You really started something when you introduced me to Pete Southerland."

His smile remained. "I know potential when I see it," he joked.

"Just think of it"—she spun from his arms— "all the studies I've wanted to complete—they're really going to happen. I can *do* something to save the lakes, not just dream about it." She looked to the heavens and her voice dropped to a whisper. "I wish Grandpa had lived to see this."

Ethan caught her hand and brought her back to his arms and they watched a shooting star race across the inky sky. "We're not really alone out here, you know."

"Ethan, when did you become such a romantic?"

"Well, I don't know if I call it romantic . . . eerie, maybe. You'll think I'm crazy, but that big old bird up there is spying on us. Again. It watched me make a fool of myself in the boat, the day we first met. And he's back now. Pulling guard duty, I guess." Lily craned her neck to see to the top of the Spruce.

Loon Lake's sentinel blue heron directed his long, pointy beak down toward the pair beneath his perch.

"Sam," Lily called out, "you can go back to the swamp. I'm fine." The big bird ruffled his feathers and lifted one foot from its perch. "Better than fine. In love!"

Sam's wings flapped against the night's dewy air. Bits of dried bark floated downward as he lifted from his perch and whooshed across Greensly Bay, leaving Lily happily wrapped in the arms of the man she loved.